I0594116

THE
MISSING
LINK

THE MISSING LINK

A JOHANNA HUDSON MYSTERY

R. FRANKLIN JAMES

CAVEL PRESS

Kenmore, WA

A Camel Press book published by Epicenter Press

Epicenter Press
6524 NE 181st St.
Suite 2
Kenmore, WA 98028

For more information go to:
www.Camelpress.com
www.Coffeetownpress.com
www.Epicenterpress.com
www.rfranklinjames.com

All rights reserved. No part of this book may be reproduced or transmitted in any form or by any means, electronic or mechanical, including photocopying, recording, or any information storage and retrieval system, without permission in writing from the publisher.

This is a work of fiction. Names, characters, places, brands, media, and incidents are either the product of the author's imagination or are used fictitiously.

Cover design by Scott Book
Interior design by Melissa Vail Coffman

The Missing Link
Copyright © 2024 by R. Franklin James

Library of Congress Control Number: 2024931754

ISBN: 978-1-68492-300-7 (Trade Paper)
ISBN: 978-1-68492-301-4 (eBook)

To Kennedy Watkins, an author in-waiting.

ACKNOWLEDGMENTS

As I ease into my Chapter Two, I have enjoyed a lineup of support that has made it a journey more than worth travelling.

First, I cannot go a single step without walking up to Jennifer McCord. She has stood by me and more importantly my work, for over a decade—there are not enough thanks. I also must acknowledge Phil Garrett and the dedication of the Camel Press publishing team that have brought my books to light.

A boundless thank you to my critique group: Kathleen Asay, Cindy Sample and Karen Phillips. They lift me with care and use their "reader" skills and knowledge to bring a richness and life to everything I write. Our critique group recently lost a member, Pat Foulk, and we are less without her.

And always, always, always I have those who continue to root for me: Patsy Williams, Penny Manson, Geri Nibbs, Carol Oliveira, and Margaret Helgeson. They inspire, support and make me smile. Thank you.

CHAPTER ONE

JOHANNA HUDSON UNLOCKED THE FRONT DOOR and sniffed at the smell of fresh paint. The landlord kept his word and finished the renovation work over the weekend. Legacy Consultants' new offices would not be considered luxurious except when compared to what they had before. Thanks to a couple of client bonus payments earlier that year, they were now financially secure enough to exchange their second floor 3-room lease, for the fourth floor. This new workplace had a small reception lobby, three workplaces, a combination space for business machines and a break room—a modest upgrade.

Her office, while slightly smaller than her partner Ava Lowell's, had a coveted view of the Hayward Hills and if she stood on her toes, she could see a sliver of the San Francisco south bay. Ava didn't mind losing the vista. She was rarely in her office, preferring to be in the "field" doing research. Her background as an archaeologist brought immense benefit to Legacy's genealogical investigations.

Johanna took a peek into the office of their new associate, Trinidad Owens. It was the closest room to the front reception area with the only window facing the hallway. The space was painted a subdued gray containing a medium-sized desk, a sole bookcase already full of books, and a slate gray and black herringbone area rug under an overstuffed gray tweed chair. Johanna sighed. It was pretty neutral and bland. Until a few months ago this room would have been filled with flowers and brilliant artifacts. Now, as Trinidad would say, it reflected her heart. The recent death of Trinidad's friend, and Legacy's unofficial driver had brought a cloud. His killing and Trinidad's own near-death hospitalization, had submerged the young woman into a "dark place" from which she had not yet recovered.

Still, every so often, Johanna would catch a glimmer of the old Trinidad that had not totally slipped away. She smiled at the small but empty cerulean blue vase that sat defiantly in the corner on the window ledge.

Next she headed to her own desk. She had come in early to get a jump on two new clients. Since the news headlines of Legacy's involvement in the solving of a high profile murder a few months past, their business had blossomed and they had turned the corner into profitability. Unfortunately, it hadn't translated into the elimination of tedious day-to-day responsibility for administrative chores. This morning required setting-up new client folders and creating online data files.

Ever since Trinidad had taken on an associate's role, they each were doing their own clerical work and shared receptionist duties. Johanna and Ava had finally come to the conclusion they were going to have to hire someone for the front desk.

"I don't like to do the paperwork," Ava said shaking her head. "And you don't like to do it. And I'm not about to ask Trinidad to revert back to her old clerical duties. So we are going to need to hire someone—maybe a temp."

They had left it at that, but Johanna knew it was time to do something, especially after she had spent a half hour pulling out the printer's misplaced staples on client files.

"Ah, good morning Johanna," Trinidad said taking her jacket off at the same time. "What time did you arrive? I thought I was getting here before anyone. What are you doing? Did you mess up the printer again?"

Named after her homeland, this morning Trinidad's silky, wavy black hair was pulled into its usual thick mid-back braid. The young woman's creamy *café au lait* complexion was set off by light brown eyes and a generous smile. She took a seat in Johanna's office.

"Good morning," she said. "But evidently I didn't get here early enough. All my extra time has gone into making up files."

Johanna re-stapled a client intake card to a folder.

Trinidad looked on. "It takes some getting used to, but you'll get the hang of it. Remember, I had to make up files and find a missing person. If I could do it, you can do it."

"Thanks Trinidad for the vote of confidence." Johanna gave her a wry smile. "So, why are you here so early?"

This morning her friend was wearing what was apparently becoming her pseudo-uniform of navy-blue pants-suit and white blouse. The blouse varied in style but not in color. The recurring outfit appeared to be a homage to her grief. Johanna often thought Trinidad had lost her footing as a person.

"Yes, good news. I think I have my first by myself client," Trinidad smiled proudly and spoke with the remnants of a patois accent. "Yes, she contacted us online and she wants us to do a family tree. I talk at . . . with her and sent her the contract on Friday. Today I see if she will sign it."

"Does it sound pretty standard?"

Trinidad tilted her head in an unasked question.

Johanna rephrased, "Does it sound simple or average?"

"Oh yes. It is standard."

Trinidad's English classes were working out well. Just every so often, it was good to double check to ensure the understanding was mutual.

Johanna glanced at the time.

"I'm ready for a break. I'm going to the cart. Can I bring you back some coffee?"

"No, I'm fine," Trinidad said. "I'll be glad when our kitchen is working and we don't have to go to the truck. Don't forget the workers will be here tomorrow to finish the infrastructure."

Johanna glanced up quickly and grinned. "Infrastructure, my goodness such a big word."

Trinidad beamed. "I looked it up when the leasing people were here last week. They used it when they talked about all the electricity and plumbing we needed—the infrastructure."

"Very well then, I'll leave you with whatever infrastructure we have," Johanna said, putting her wallet and phone in her coat pocket. "I'm going to the food truck before the coffee line gets any longer."

OUTSIDE, SHE SLOWED HER PACE AND frowned. She sensed she was someone's focus. Without turning her head, she saw a man out of the corner of her eye standing across the street staring at her. He held onto a sign of well-used bent cardboard: "Will Work For Food." She kept her gaze forward.

The food truck had a long winding line this morning. Evidently the "infrastructure" was out in several other offices in the building. When her turn came, Johanna ordered two cups of coffee and two donuts. She walked across the street to her observer.

Seeing her approach, the man tightened his grip on the sign, but continued to stare at her.

"Here?" She reached out with the bag. "Would you like some coffee and a couple of donuts?"

He was tall and thin, wearing at least three sets of flannel shirts and a once tan, now multi grime looking trench coat. His face and hands were smudged, and his dark hair oily, still Johanna could tell he was young.

Without hesitation, he set the sign on the ground next to a weathered backpack. Grasping the bag he took out the coffee, drank deeply, and then practically inhaled a donut. He avoided looking directly at her, but she could see from the glances he stole, his blue eyes held intelligence and clarity.

"Thank you." He took another long drink.

"You're welcome." She turned to walk back to the building.

"I . . . I know who you are."

Johanna turned and frowned. "What?"

He took a step forward, then when he saw Johanna's expression of alarm, took the step back. "Yeah, I was the one who was there when you were rescued at the BART maintenance yard."

Her breathing quickened. His words transported her to a flashback from a few months past. Johanna had been kidnapped and had barely escaped except for the help from a homeless man—apparently this homeless man.

"You!" Johanna exclaimed. "You were the one who saved me. I always wanted to thank you. Did the police tell you I wanted to thank you?"

He tilted his head with a smirk. "No, lady, the cops didn't tell me anything except to get my stuff off of BART property."

"I'm sorry," she said. "I did, and I do, want to thank you for actually saving my life."

He looked down at his battered tennis shoes. "You're welcome."

There was an awkward silence. The coffee line at the cart had gotten longer.

"Well, I need to get back to work." Johanna took out her wallet. "Look, here's thirty-dollars. It's all the cash I have. I can meet you somewhere tomorrow with more. I know it's a small thank you for all you did to help me."

He took the money and shoved it in his coat pocket.

"Not more cash. You can really thank me by giving me a job."

"What? I don't have a need for a . . . a . . . a person. We're an office. We need clerical and administrative skills."

He straightened and ran a hand over his head, moving his thick dark hair from off his forehead.

"I . . . I read about you and the killings in the newspaper. I went to the library. They let me in if I . . . if I stay invisible." He looked past her. "I wanted to know about you . . . who you were, and uh, where you worked." He once more looked down at his battered tennis shoes.

"You mean you were waiting for me this morning?" Johanna stiffened.

"Yeah, but not in a weird way," he sighed. "Look, I can do office work," he rushed on. "I used to work as an intern for an insurance company."

Johanna groaned. *How did she get into this, even more how could she get out?*

"I don't know." She looked over her shoulder, shaking her head. Then grudgingly, "Well, we do need a receptionist, someone who—"

"Who will greet customers and . . . bring them coffee while they're waiting . . . and know how to use a computer and a desk phone," he said. "I know I don't look it right now." His hands smoothed his grubby coat lapels. "But I can do those things."

Johanna sighed. "Uh, we're looking for someone with education maybe even some college."

He grimaced with disbelief. "You want a college degree for a receptionist. How much do you pay?"

"You're right." Johanna had to chuckle. "I guess I . . . I'm just—"

"Just afraid of hiring a homeless person who could be on drugs, or an escaped prisoner, or a burglar, or even worse. Well, I'm not any of those things. I'm just going through a streak of bad luck and you could end it for me. You could save my life, like I saved yours."

Now that hit home.

Resigned, Johanna took a card from her wallet. "Our building is across the street. But then, you probably already know that. Here's our suite number. We're having some building work done today and tomorrow, but if you could come for an interview on Wednesday at 9:00 a.m., we'll see if there is a fit."

He nodded repeatedly and picking up his sack started to walk determinedly down the sidewalk turning to look back at Johanna with a tentative smile.

"Wait," she called out.

He returned to where she stood. "Yes?"

"What's your name?"

He gave her an odd look.

"I thought you were going to tell me you had changed your mind. No one has asked me for my name in a long time." He paused. "It's Marty . . . Martin Blake."

She nodded and watched him disappear around the corner.

"YOU DID WHAT?" AVA AND TRINIDAD said in unison.

Johanna cringed. "No need to overreact. I didn't hire him; I only said he could have an interview."

"But Johanna," Ava shook her head. "What possessed you to even give him hope? Now he'll always be hanging around, maybe even bring his friends in growing numbers to beg in front of the building for an easy touch."

"Ava, he did save my life."

"I know but—"

Trinidad raised her hand. "Ava and Johanna, this man is coming here; there is nothing we can do. We cannot call him to not come. He will be here Wednesday morning. I will be with Johanna so she will be safe."

"Thanks, Trinidad, I'd like that," Johanna said. She then turned to Ava. "It's common courtesy and the least I could do."

"Hmmm," Ava responded. "Let's hope we don't regret it."

TRINIDAD

TRINIDAD WASN'T NERVOUS.

Okay, yes she was, but it was a good nervous. Her first client and her first official chance to prove herself. Simone Griffin had a very nice voice on the phone, and Trinidad could tell she had manners and education. And for good measure, Trinidad had made sure during a comprehensive public records search that

Simone wasn't wanted by the law nor had any legal actions filed against her.

It never hurt to be careful.

They were meeting in Ava's office. Trinidad thought it best to impress Ms. Griffin with the full weight of the company's best furnishings.

"I didn't know if you wanted me to bring all my papers, or just enough to get you started." Griffin said.

"Ah, Simone, can I call you Simone?" Trinidad requested. "And you must call me Trinidad. I just wanted you to see from our offices that we are a serious business. In the future I will come to you, or we will meet someplace convenient."

"Sure, please call me Simone. Oh, and no problem coming here. I work in the field a lot—on calls." Simone took out a sheet of paper from a folder and slid it across the top of the desk. "I filled out the tree chart from online. I brought it with me. As you can see, I don't know much past my grandmother on my mother's side and nothing on my father's."

Trinidad glanced quickly at the largely empty boxes on the form. She took a longer gaze at the young woman in front of her. From her own research, she knew Simone was a divorcee. What she couldn't tell from her research was that the plain looking girl had poorly dyed her own hair a deep tin-look auburn. She also had dark circles under brown eyes and looked twenty years older than her birth certificate age of twenty-six.

"Families are funny things. Each one is different," Trinidad said folding her hands on the desk. "Now tell me why you are curious about your family. Are you doing research to satisfy family ancestor tales? Genealogy is like a living mystery."

"No, none of those things." Simone moistened her lips. "I'm dying."

CHAPTER TWO

"**Y**OU SAY YOUR CLIENT IS DYING?" Johanna asked Trinidad, setting her cup down on the counter behind her in Legacy's small kitchen. Their file boxes were stacked against the wall and on the table there was no room to spread out.

"Let's move this discussion to the conference room," Ava said, already walking down the hall. "Trinidad, what does your client expect you to do?"

That afternoon, they were having their first office case-meeting since they moved. Johanna had stipulated the time be used to go over all the client files that were being worked on so they could be a resource for each other. They had already been at it for an hour when they looked to their new associate for her answer. Trinidad pulled her chair closer to the round table and pulled out a thick pad of paper.

"I know, I asked the same thing." She turned to a page filled with notes and read slowly, "Her name is Simone Griffin. She says she has hereditary hemochromatosis." Trinidad looked up into their puzzled looks. "It is a disease when the body builds up too much iron in the skin and in the organs it can cause major damage and complications."

"Sounds miserable," Ava frowned.

"It is. I looked it up," Trinidad said. "It is a rare disease. A person has to inherit two mutant genes, one from each parent."

"And she wants you to . . ." Johanna raised her eyebrows in a question.

"Here is the tricky part," Trinidad sighed. "She was tested by her doctor and learned she had the disease. But the people she thought were her parents did not have the gene. Well, her mother had the gene—but not the man she thought was her father."

"What does the mother say?" Ava asked. "Does this mean the man Simone Griffin thought was her father is not?"

"Was not," Trinidad said. "He passed away five years ago, along with her mother. They were in a car accident."

"So-o-o?" Johanna dragged.

"So, she had a locket of her mother's hair and a brush she kept of her father's. Her cousin, or a young man she thinks is her cousin, works in a forensic lab for the Sheriff's department. She got him to run the test for her on his own time. When he did, that is when she discovered the man she thought was her father did not have the gene and therefore could not be her real father."

"Wow," Ava said, Ava leaning heavily to the back of her chair. "In a way, in a sad way, it's a good thing her parents aren't here. I wouldn't want to have that conversation."

Johanna agreed and got up to refill her mug. "I take it she wants you to build her family tree from her mother's side, hoping to find her father?"

Trinidad nodded.

"When I meet her I could tell she is a nice young lady—quiet and polite. We got along well," Trinidad said. "She wants me to build her tree and find her real father's identity." She flipped to the next page in her pad. "There is one branch I can start to pull. Her grandmother is also dead but she has a great-aunt, who lives in San Jose. Simone says she does not remember much about her. She has pictures of her mother's sisters—her aunts. They are holding Simone when she was a baby. The aunts and Simone have not seen each other since she was a child. Simone doesn't have a lot of money, so I told her we would go as far as we could. This is my first client," Trinidad said. "I have to try."

"I agree," Ava said.

"Then it's settled." Johanna smiled, raising her mug. "To your first client."

AVA

AVA SAT STARING AT THE BLINKING cursor on her laptop screen. The informal-formal "staff meeting" had ended, and everyone had returned to their offices. She stared at the email, once more re-read the offer and typed her response. If she hit "send" her life could change forever or at least for the next two years. To work in Australia where she had trained and made her reputation as a renowned archaeologist was an opportunity she did not seek, nor expect. She would fill the role of Finds Manager on one of the world's most prominent archaeological dig teams.

But what about Legacy?

The last months had been tumultuous and somewhat of an upheaval, but the company had not only survived, it had thrived. At one point, she was the only one able to keep the business going. Johanna and Trinidad had, and to some extent, were still going through various stages of recovery, emotional as well as physical.

Could she leave them?

The dig site was adjacent to the famous Cranebrook Terrace indigenous findings in New South Wales. The site director had assured her she would have blocks of time to return to the States between cataloging, that they would accommodate her American interests. But she knew herself too well. Once the dig was under-way the intensity and momentum would take over and she would be confronted with being torn—a foot in both camps.

The cursor blinked back at her.

CHAPTER THREE

JOHANNA CONSIDERED THE WILD ROSE CAFÉ her office away
from the office. It was usually easier to meet her clients there
with its easy access off the MacArthur Freeway and being a couple
of blocks from the Pleasanton BART Station. Fortunately, Rhonda,
the owner was very accommodating and, except for replacement
coffee pours, allowed her to sit undisturbed if Johanna had a client
with her.

Today, it was the café's lull time between the breakfast and lunch
crowd. The aroma of pancakes and bacon mingled with hamburg-
ers and fries. She had taken the table toward the rear of the diner
with a window on the street. The young woman across from her
was frantically looking through her tote, pulling out a wallet, keys,
perfume, sunglasses, a second pair of sunglasses, a thin hardback
book, packet of tissues and a phone—and she wasn't halfway down.
Johanna watched mesmerized as the woman held onto the bag with
one hand and shoveled items out with the other. She was attractive,
of an indeterminate age. Her left slender ring finger sported a brilliant solitaire. Her deep blue eyes and dark brown hair were set off
with pouty lips that were clearly familiar with collagen injections.

"Since this is just our first meeting, Leslie," Johanna said, reaching for the sleek gold Mont Blanc pen that was ready to roll off the

table. She put it on top of the growing stack of items. "Maybe we can talk about your family search first and you can show me any . . . any background documentation later."

Leslie Todd didn't look up. "A lot of good this meeting will be if you don't see—ah, here it is." Leslie smoothed out a folded paper and set it in front of Johanna.

As she gave an initial glance to the form, Leslie returned all items to her bag with a wide swoop of her arm.

"I see this is your birth certificate." She looked up. "Is there a problem?"

"Oh, yeah," Leslie replied. "There's a problem all right. It's a fake."

"A fake," Johanna repeated. "What's the matter?" She peered at the entries. "Aren't you Leslie Todd? Aren't these your parents?"

"Oh, they're my parents, but they're not real." She tapped the table-top. "More importantly I'm not real."

"I don't understand," Johanna said, puzzled.

"It's okay, I don't blame you. I don't understand it either." The woman sighed. "I'll start from what I do know. My parents both died skiing in an avalanche when I was five. I was raised by my grandparents, my mother's parents, who divorced when I was fifteen. At that point, I lived with my grandmother until I left for college. She died several years ago." She paused, shaking her head in remembrance. "I was curious, that's all. I'd signed up for this family research site . . . because I wanted to explore my family tree. It sounded like fun."

She rubbed her eyes with her fingertips.

"Anyway, I started with my mother. I put in her name. Nothing. There was nothing. Then I entered the name of the woman I thought was my grandmother, the address where she said we lived after my parents died—all nothing. I was frustrated but not deterred, at least not yet. Then I tried tracking my Mom's social security number—after waiting over an hour with that ridiculous music, and then another back and forth with the department representative, she finally said it didn't exist. I would have to go into the office to find out anything more."

Johanna raised her eyebrows. "That is strange."

"Strange isn't the word," Leslie said. "I did the same thing for my father and got the same thing—nothing. No verified social security identification at all."

Johanna's mind raced with the possibilities and the ramifications, none she thought would be reassuring, so she remained silent and let her client continue. The once self-assured individual was slowly losing her confidence.

Leslie played with her glass of water, twisting it on the wet napkin.

"Then I thought to put in the information from where I grew up and went to school. It was online. I was in their alumni files. At least I wasn't crazy." Leslie shook her head and took a sip from her glass. "I found this copy of my birth certificate in family files where my parents had kept important papers, but then . . . but then when I couldn't trace anything back, something told me to order an original of my birth certificate from the county. You know the one with the embossed stamp?"

Johanna nodded slowly.

The woman's eyes glistened with tears. She swiped at them. "I wasn't in the system. They had no birth certificate for me."

"Wait, did you ever apply for a driver's license? A passport?"

"I took the birth certificate copy I had to the DMV. They accepted it—no questions. I've never applied for a passport."

"What about your job? Didn't you have to have a Social Security card? How do you pay taxes?"

Tears were now flowing down Leslie's cheeks.

"Listen to me. I didn't think about it. I always thought my parents ordered my social security number when I was born. I've used it all my life. I'm only . . . uh, thirty-two. My official social security card was included in my parents' files my grandmother kept. I took it out for my job and human resources. I don't carry it around with me. There was never a question. But . . . but—"

"But you took it to the Social Security Office and they said it was invalid," Johanna said quietly. "They told you that you would never be able to collect benefits with that number. Your W2 was enough for the IRS to accept your returns and payments, and you've been living under the radar."

"Yes . . . yes."

Leslie choked back a sob and Johanna motioned to Rhonda for their check. They needed privacy. Minutes later they were sitting in a nearby neighborhood greenspace on a concrete bench under a leafy locust tree.

"It's going to be all right." Johanna put her arm around the thin shoulder. "I'll help you. It may take a little time—"

"I can pay you. My family left me a lot of money."

"Money won't make things go faster. Research can take a while, and we have hourly rates." She turned to look the young woman in the eyes. "Leslie, did you ever consider there is a reason why your parents' and your identity are . . . are buried?"

She nodded.

"I want to know, Johanna. I want to know who I really am for my own peace of mind." She waved her ring. "I'm engaged. But my fiancé thinks this is just digging up trouble. He says it doesn't matter to him, he wants me to drop it. But it matters to me. I want to know my real family tree, even if it's just my parent's real names." She slumped in resignation.

Johanna had a sinking feeling the reveal of her family tree might not be one to bring her much peace of mind.

"BEFORE I TAKE LESLIE TODD ON, I wanted to run it by you two." Johanna said relaying her conversation to Ava and Trinidad that afternoon.

They were all in the conference room while the workers finished up in the break room.

"I will help you with this one, Johanna. It sounds interesting," Trinidad offered. "It would be like working with a missing person, who did not know they were missing."

"Ordinarily, I'd like to work with you on this one as well," Ava mused. "But. . ."

"But you have bigger challenges," Johanna said.

Ava looked hesitant. "I'm not altogether sure that—"

"We promise not to do anything to damage our brand until you get back." Johanna teased.

Ava rolled her eyes.

"Yes, Ava," Trinidad added. "Johanna told me about your job offer. We will keep Legacy strong until you return,"

"I keep thinking about what happened the last time I left just six months ago," Ava responded. "Back less than four hours, I was attacked by one of your new clients."

Johanna waved her hand. "Admittedly, it was a terrible incident, but things worked out in the end—eventually." She grinned. "Ava, you know you don't want to pass on this dig appointment. Go— we'll be fine. Maybe you can find us some clients in Australia while you're over there."

"She is right," Trinidad jumped in. "My cousin Lincoln has relatives near Sydney. I will tell them you are coming. They will welcome you."

Ava shook her head. "Ah, that's okay, Trini. I—"

"Not a problem." Trinidad waved her hand. "I will do."

Johanna did a fair job of hiding her chuckle after seeing Ava's look of anxiousness. "Trinidad, aren't Lincoln's relatives, your relatives?"

"Yes, they are my relatives too, but Lincoln is a man and is a bigger deal." She shrugged. "They will take better care of you if you use his name."

"Well, fortunately I've been on digs in Sydney before," Ava said. Then hastily added when she saw Trinidad's frown, "But you can never have too many acquaintances in a foreign land."

"I must go now," Trinidad said glancing at the time on her phone. "I am picking up research documents I ordered at the Family

History Center. I will be back tomorrow in time for the interview with Martin Blake."

She dashed to her office, grabbed her purse and jacket and, with a wave, she was out the front door.

Johanna and Ava were both quiet. They sipped their coffee in silence.

"I'm waiting," Ava said.

"For what?"

"I know what you're thinking," Ava said, leaning forward. "I'm going to come back. You think I won't, but I will. It's just my vanity won't let me turn my back on a field title at a significant dig."

"You should go. I want you to go, I mean it. You'll be impossible to work with if you don't." Johanna tipped up her mug to finish her coffee. "When are you leaving?"

"Not for three weeks. They want me in four, but it gives me a week to catch up with the dig. I'll still have time to wrap up most of my clients, and with the few left over I'll give Trinidad some research to do and she can run my remaining trees by you." Ava smiled. "My phase of the excavation should take about four, maybe five months."

Johanna got up and rinsed out her cup. "Three weeks, we'll be ready."

CHAPTER FOUR

Trinidad had set up three metal folding chairs and a small makeshift table in front of the office receptionist counter.

Johanna looked up from her seat at the clock on the wall. Blake had five minutes, after that she would be justified in excluding him as an applicant. Ava, as usual, was right. She had let her soft heart get ahead of her.

At four minutes to nine o'clock, the front door opened.

It was clear Martin Blake had paid a visit to a second-hand store. He had showered and smelled of Ivory soap. While his tan Dockers and white polo shirt were clean and pressed, they hung loosely on his thin frame. His face was sunburned, but he had tamed his dark brown hair into a decent cut and it framed his face with a side part and a little length in the back.

Trinidad walked up to him with an extended hand. He took it, even as his glance went to Johanna who gave him an encouraging smile from her seat.

"Hello, come in," Trinidad said.

"Marty, glad you could make it. This is our associate, Trinidad," Johanna said. She pointed to the third chair. "Please sit. Can we get you anything?"

Sitting, he shook his head. She couldn't help but notice his right knee was doing a rapid staccato.

"Well, why don't we give you an idea about what's required for the position," Johanna said. "And then you can tell us about your . . . ah skills."

He looked from one to the other, and biting down on his bottom lip, nodded.

Johanna used the next few minutes to go over their business and what they needed an office receptionist to do.

"Now, can you describe your background for us?"

"My background," Marty cleared his throat. "Um . . . I'm from El Cerrito and I went to Oakland Tech. I did graduate. I have a single Mom . . . somewhere. My counselor got me a job out of high school with Bestway Insurance as an intern on the front desk. They liked me because I worked hard and kept the customers entertained until an agent would meet with them." He looked down at his hands. "They went out of business about a year ago, so I lost my job. I couldn't bring home money anymore. We had to move, my Mom left and I was on my own."

"Is that when you had to live on the street?" Trinidad asked.

He nodded, tapping his fingers on his jittering knee.

"Marty, we need someone who can answer the phone, monitor emails, set up client folders and our files. We will require absolute confidentiality." Johanna spoke slowly trying to calm his agitation. "Do you know computers?"

"Yes, I used them at Bestway and we had them in school." His face turned even redder under his burn. "I know . . . I know I don't look like much. But I can do this. I'm a quick learner. I just need a chance. I just—"

"You have the job," Trinidad said solemnly.

Johanna jerked her head around to send Trinidad a wide-eyed pointed stare.

Trinidad ignored her.

"What!" Marty grinned, his leg stilled.

"Johanna and I will talk about the details," Trinidad went on. "How can we reach you?"

He rubbed his hands along his thighs.

"Er . . . couldn't I just come back here to hear what you have to say? I don't . . . I don't have a phone right now." Marty's eyes were downcast. "And I don't really care about the work details."

Johanna exchanged another look with Trinidad.

"Marty, I feel you are a good person. I think I know someone who might be able to help you," Trinidad said. "Let us check on a couple of things. Come back this afternoon about four o'clock."

TRINIDAD

TRINIDAD KNEW SHE HAD TO ADDRESS Johanna's list of concerns, but she had no trouble convincing Reverend George Monroe to allow Marty to stay in the little room at the back of Three Crosses Church.

"Ah, Trinidad Owens, it is good to see you again," he said in patois. "I read about you in the papers. I am sorry about your friend who was killed last year. How can I help you?"

"I can speak English good now, Reverend. Yes, it was sad about my friend." Her voice lowered then she raised her chin. "It is good to see you, too. I'm here because I need help for someone."

She quickly explained Marty Blake's situation.

"Hmm, you are still extending care to others," the Reverend said. "I must tell you the publicity the church received from our last encounter brought a surplus in donations, and we were able to take care of much of our deferred maintenance."

Trinidad gave him a questioning look.

"*Entretien différé*." He smiled when she nodded understanding. "Anyway, we owe much to you and Legacy Consultants. I think we may be able to help this young man for a short while."

Trinidad grinned. "Thank you so much, Reverend Monroe. This is good news for someone I think will be able to turn his life around. I will send him to you."

"That's fine." The Reverend crossed his arms and took a step back. "I must say you look very sophisticated now, Trinidad, and not so much the look of our country's island culture. Where are your colors?" He peered at her. "Is everything alright with you? Your clothes and English are impressive, but the look in your eyes seems *blessée*."

"Wounded?" Trinidad said looking past him. "I . . . I am good, but not the same as before. I fit in better with my new life now. I am getting on to the future and letting go of the past."

"Hmm, curious, the past helps us to remember events in context and to be grateful for the learning and people it provided. We don't have to let it go to remember who we really are, but maybe it should be considered another tool in our box."

Trinidad shrugged off his words with a chuckle.

"Reverend, my English isn't that good yet to understand everything you just said. But it sounds interesting." She looked at her phone. "I must go. I have an errand to run before I go back to the office and give Marty the good news."

"Come back soon and visit our service. We also have one or two support groups you might benefit from."

"I'll try."

He gave her a long look. "Hmm, 'try', now that's an interesting word."

CHAPTER FIVE

"**N**ICK, HOW WOULD I FIND OUT if a person was in a witness protection program?"

Johanna and Detective Dominic "Nick" Quinn were drinking steaming cups of coffee and sharing an oversized aromatic cinnamon roll as their quick makeshift breakfast at the Wild Rose Café. Their relationship would likely be classified somewhere between the "to be determined" category and friends with benefits. Over the last couple of years, it was evident to both that they enjoyed each other's company and equally important each other's deductive abilities.

"Oh, no, what are you up to now?" He said. "You know, your business is sounding more and more like a missing person's service than a genealogy research enterprise," He said, catching an errant crumb on his lip with his napkin. "Think about what you're asking, Johanna, the whole idea of having a witness protection program is so you can't find people."

"I know, but suppose they're dead?"

His brow wrinkled and he ran his hand through his thick dark hair. She had gotten to know well that gesture over the past months. They had been thrown together on a couple of law enforcement matters in the past that Nick still insisted should never have involved Johanna. She could tell he was wary to say more, not knowing if she would use his answer to get into trouble.

She smiled to herself. Not only was he physically tall, lean and as her grandmother would say, easy on the eye. Nick took his job as Managing Detective in the Investigative Division with the Sheriff's department seriously, and he made Johanna feel protected. But at the moment she could tell by his clipped choice of vocabulary that he was definitely on guard.

"The witness protection program is run by the U.S. Marshalls Service. California also has a protection program that's a smaller version for crimes not covered by the Feds," he said, his gaze probing hers. "You could start there, but I can tell you to expect an uphill battle." He offered an engaging smile. "Why don't you tell me exactly what your client wants to know? Maybe I can help you."

It was her turn to go on guard.

"No, not necessary, I don't want to waste your time." She leaned forward. "All I'm hoping for is you point me in the right direction. While there's a lot my client doesn't know about her background, I can still go after a couple of possible leads," Johanna said retrieving a small notebook from her purse. "But since you insist, I'll tell you what we have."

Without providing the name, she quickly took him through Todd's search attempts and meager background results.

Nick shook his head. "Do you ever get any easy customers? Ones who have straightforward ancestry requests, or is it too late and word has gotten out that Legacy Consultants is where the last resort cases go?"

"Very funny," Johanna laughed along with him. Although, she had a fleeting thought he might be right. "But this is an easy one. She just wants to know 'who' she is. She doesn't have a criminal background. And, I should say I haven't mentioned the possibility of witness protection to her. I wanted to check it out first. She's feeling spooked enough as it is."

"Well, if she's in the protection program, there is some criminal activity somewhere along the way, likely affecting one or both her parents, or maybe even her grandparents." He took out his phone and glanced down at the screen. "I've got to go. Tell you what, I've got a friend who's married to a U.S. Marshall let me see if I can discover what options or steps your client can take. Frankly, I'm not sure if you can even find out if your client is in the protection program."

He stood and laid some cash on the table.

She looked up at him. "Can you call him today?"

"What makes you think it's a 'him'?" He grinned. "But yes, I will call him when I get to my office."

"Thank you." Johanna laughed, and then turned serious. "And Nick, thank you too for the talk and . . . the breakfast."

They traded appreciative looks. He gave her a short bow before turning to leave.

TRINIDAD

MARTY WAS SITTING IN THE BUILDING'S LOBBY when Trinidad rushed the double doors and pointed him to the elevator. She unlock the office door. No one else was in and it was dark.

She turned on the various lights.

"Why are you being so nice to me?" he said.

"You came to us for a job. We have a job," Trinidad said, taking off her jacket and hanging it on the coat rack near the front door. "More important, you saved Johanna's life from a killer and that means you get A-plus treatment." She paused, looking him in the eyes. "We are more grateful to you than you can imagine."

Clearing her throat of the sudden emotion that rose up, she pointed him to the space behind the receptionist counter.

"This is your office." She motioned to the cubical desk and chair behind the counter.

He came around and sat in the swivel chair.

"Great, this is fine." He gave her a broad grin. He opened the laptop and tapped on the screen. "Good, the appointment spreadsheet file is already open; I'm familiar with this program." He picked up the phone. "I just need to know whose phone extension in the office belongs to whom."

"I am glad you find the easiest part of the job, easy," Trinidad said "Now, I will show you how to put on the coffee and hot water for tea. Come with me." She waited for him to stand and follow her. "You must do this the first thing when you come in."

Marty responded with nods as she quickly took him through the motions in the break room. They returned to the front desk. Trinidad pulled up a chair and reaching over the keyboard used the mouse to move the cursor over the screen.

"Okay, now to go through how to set up the files. This will require more . . . more thought on your part."

"I'm ready." Marty nodded and then he tilted his head. "By the way, where is your accent from?"

"Trinidad Tobago."

"Of course, the name." he grinned. "Okay, let's do this, where do I start?"

Trinidad spent the next thirty minutes going through Legacy's office procedures and operations. She reiterated how the files were critical to correctly tracking the bits and pieces of information as they came in.

"One day we pick up a file with all its bits and pieces, put them together, and keep searching until we unravel the history of a family," Trinidad said. Leading him back to her office.

"Like a trail of crumbs," Marty responded.

"Crumbs?"

"Never mind." He smiled. "Just thank you. What time do you want me here tomorrow?"

"Your works hours are eight-thirty to five-thirty, with an hour for lunch—Monday through to Friday." Trinidad reached inside her pocket and handed him the Reverend's business card. "Now, I have made arrangements for you to be here—I mean to live here," she said noticing his eyes widen and then glisten. She looked away.

"It is a community church with a housing unit available. I think it is a good place for you to start over."

He stared at her, then blinked at the card. He stood and put his arms around her shoulders giving a strong squeeze.

Trinidad stiffened, her arms at her sides.

"Enough please. There is a lot of work to do." She took a step back. "Starting today, I will continue to train you."

He dropped his arms and backed up.

"I'm sorry if . . . but nobody . . . thank you, I . . . this means . . ."

"There is no need to keep saying thank you. You are very welcome, Marty."

She picked up papers from the desk and began to separate them into stacks. She didn't look up at the retreating figure until she heard the whirr of the start-up of the computer. A soft smile crossed her face.

AVA

AVA DEBATED GETTING UP AND LEAVING, but she noticed she hadn't moved from the restaurant chair.

Her ex-husband, Eric Lowell, had once been the love of her life. Unfortunately, she'd soon discovered he was also the love of many other lives. "But, I only loved and married you," he proclaimed when she confronted him with divorce papers, causing her to wonder why she had been so cursed. She could, and did, often kick herself for needing his help several months back to bail out Legacy when they were struggling with finances. Actually, he hadn't bailed them out as much as repaid what he owed.

And now, here he was again. After his prolonged begging and promising her he didn't want anything from her, she'd reluctantly agreed to meet him for coffee at the salad bar a couple of blocks from Legacy offices. She had no intention of eating, but it gave Eric an opportunity to reveal his latest urgency then she could quickly return to her job after telling him "no."

He'd chosen a table in the rear, next a window.

"Look, I just want to say thank you for meeting with me. You're a far better friend to me than I am to you. But, I need this small favor." He put on an exaggerated sad face. "You know my parents don't have a lot of faith in me, and rightly so I admit." His hand shot up to halt her retort. "But they gave me this one last shot to be responsible, and I can't disappoint them again."

"But you are irresponsible."

"Thank you, Ava, for your confidence," he said with sarcasm. "Years ago I wouldn't have bothered trying to show how I could change, but I can . . . I am. My Mom, who still adores you by the way, asked me to deliver a family heirloom to her sister in Hawaii. I told Mom I would hand carry it, she doesn't trust the mail. But something's come up and I just can't leave the business right now."

"No."

"Wait," he rushed. "You don't know what I'm asking. I read about Cranebrook. I know how important this dig is to you. Even I remember how you would go on about the Cranebrook site, years ago. Now, all I need is for you to deliver my Mom's pendant to her sister during your layover in Hawaii."

"No."

Undaunted he continued, "She would be ecstatic if you would carry it. You've been to Aunt Lillian's house, she hasn't moved. She would love to see you." He tapped his side of his head with his palm. "Wait. I just thought of something. I can make it easy for you, I'll have my cousin, Matt, meet you at the airport and he can take the package to Aunt Lillian."

Ava shook her head.

She'd briefly thought she would have liked to visit with the sixty-eight year old, Bohemian and pot-smoking Aunt Lil. But the timing of the layover would be cutting it close. Her brow wrinkled. "By the way, how did you know I was going to Australia and would have a layover in Honolulu?"

He reached inside his jacket pocket and pulled out a folded newspaper printout, then handed it to her.

"This past Monday, the Chronicle did a retrospective on local Stanford grads 'where are they now?,'" he said. "They mentioned your recent appointment. And I know you only fly Qantas."

She scanned the article. Her name was listed as a participant in an historical dig starting in a few weeks. Ava didn't try to hide her irritation or the feeling he was somehow using her and maybe even spying on her. Still, the only things about Eric that she still liked were his parents. They took their break-up hard. Ava knew they had hoped she would be the one to turn their only son's life around. She had failed. She owed them.

"What's so important to your mother about this pendant?" Ava said. "You're not trying to smuggle something into Hawaii are you?"

His jaw stiffened.

"Admittedly, in the past I may not have been the most reliable person in our relationship but I don't ever remember bringing my mother or my family into any of my dealings." He paused then resumed. "You know, if I had changed would you even notice? I'm trying, Ava."

"Sorry," she said contrite. "Tell me about this jewelry."

"It's some kind of maternal line thing. It's a necklace that's been in the family for generations," Eric responded. "It passes from daughter to daughter. Mom didn't have any girls. Aunt Lil does— so she gets it. You remember my cousin Gemma, don't you?"

"No." Ava squinted trying to remember Eric's small line of cousins.

"That's right, I forgot, Gemma was at college when we visited. You never met her."

"I know I'll likely regret it, but your family has always been so good to me. Eric, you've got to promise me if I do this—and I can't leave the airport so your cousin Matt had better be there. And, I had better not be stopped by immigration or security." Ava took a deep sigh. "If I do this, you won't come back for favors, or money, or *anything* else."

Eric raised his hand. "I swear."

Ava raised her eyebrow, crossed her arms and shook her head. "That's your left hand."

CHAPTER SIX

JOHANNA SNUCK A LOOK AT LESLIE SITTING next to her. Smartly dressed, she was staring into space past a chattering group of girls near the receptionist desk in the U.S. Marshal's lobby in San Francisco. Johanna had only a vague idea of what U.S. Marshal's duties were and it wasn't until Nick mentioned the marshals could be involved with Leslie's search, that she did a little research. U.S. Marshals service is specialized, they not only protect the federal judiciary, they apprehend and house federal fugitives and prisoners, and more to the point, they operate the Witness Security Program.

"Leslie, are you okay?" she asked quietly. "We were lucky to get an appointment so quickly. Ethan Cook has agreed to talk about what happens to family members when . . . when the parents are in witness protection. Do you still want me to sit in with you? If you want privacy, I can wait here."

"What?" Leslie jerked her head up from whatever deep thought place she'd been.

"I'm saying, it was Detective Nick Quinn who arranged for this meeting." She took a deep breath. "Cook doesn't know your name. He's only providing general information." Johanna frowned. "But, he's going to need to have your complete background—whatever you know, if he's going to be able to verify your family was under protection." She moistened her lips. "You don't know me. We just met. You may not want me in the room. And, I'll understand."

Leslie's face drained of color. "No, Johanna, I want you with me. Please. You got me this far. I never thought of witness protection. There's nothing you can't hear." She clutched her hands. "I . . . I want to know and I don't want to know. I'm too nervous. I won't be able to concentrate. You'll remember what he says. When we get back to your office, and I've calmed down, I'll need you to tell me."

Johanna nodded her understanding.

ETHAN COOK WAS NOTHING LIKE JOHANNA expected. Not that the tall man, with a trim physique, dark brown skin and closely cropped hair didn't measure up to government expectations—it was his smile that went to his eyes. A smile that underscored how handsome and physically appealing he was. Leslie blinked several times and blushed. Johanna moistened her lips when she realized he had asked a question.

"Yes, yes, I'm Johanna Hudson and this is . . . is Leslie Todd," she stumbled. "Detective Nick Quinn referred us to you."

Leslie nodded eagerly, speechless.

Cook seemed amused at their fluster.

"We can talk in one of the visitor rooms," he said, not waiting for an answer and headed down a corridor of interior windowed offices.

They followed like ducklings until he pointed for them to take a seat in a room with a small table and four metal chairs.

"So, I have twenty minutes," he said, pulling a notebook from his pants pocket. "How can I help?"

"You have the most beautiful voice I have ever heard," Leslie pondered out loud.

Johanna gave a nervous smile. Cook laughed.

"Well thank you. I'll let my husband know some people like to hear me speak."

Well that ends that fantasy.

She and Leslie both straightened in their chairs.

Johanna cleared her throat. "We're here to find out what would we have to do if Miss Todd's family was included in a witness protection program. How would she get started finding out about her real past?" She turned to the young woman who also seemed to have recovered her senses. "Leslie, why don't you tell Mr. Cook what you told me."

Leslie swallowed and took the next minutes to stumble through what little she knew about her family.

"I guess, I never questioned my background until I signed up for one of those genealogy websites." She shrugged. "I could find nothing about my family. There was nothing there at all. Johanna came up with the idea of witness protection."

Cook made a quick note and then leaned back in his chair. "When someone enters the Witness Security Program they are in imminent danger and therefore their children are in danger. We are tasked with erasing every thread of information that could lead to the new identity. We create a new life and a complete background story for individuals in exchange for their testimony in criminal court."

"But the children," Johanna said. "What happens to them when they grow up?"

"Yeah, that can be a little tricky," he said. "By law, U.S. Marshals can't confirm or deny anyone's existence in the program."

"But how can I collect my Social Security or get a passport?" Leslie said her voice rising. "I feel like a non-person."

Johanna patted her hand.

"Mr. Cook, if we gave you the fake social security numbers for Leslie's parents, could you find out who they really were?" Johanna knew her voice reflected her frustration. "Or, if that doesn't help, maybe you could tell us how their protection process got started."

Ethan Cook shook his head.

"I hear both of you, but I wouldn't know where to start," he replied and motioned to Leslie. "I don't even know the state let alone the county where your parents entered the program. There is no database of protected individuals. We have nothing to do with them once they are settled. That's why the first critical rule in the program is witnesses must not make contact with former associates or unprotected family members."

"But I don't know my family members," Leslie said short of a wail. "My parents are dead."

"I'm sorry," he said sounding concerned. He looked down at the time on his phone.

Johanna scanned her brain for ideas before the meeting came to an end. She found it hard to believe somewhere out there in government land there wasn't a log of protected witnesses.

"Mr. Cook, when the witness gives testimony it's for a specific case, right? I mean there's a court out there somewhere took the testimony and determined the testimony warranted putting the witness under protection." She frowned. "It must cost a lot of money to set a family up."

"Yes, only a court can approve entering into the program, and yes, it costs quite a bit to set a family up."

"Leslie, let's go," Johanna said, picking up her purse. "Our twenty minutes are up and Mr. Cook needs to get on with his day."

Everyone stood. Leslie's dejection was obvious.

"Look, I'll tell you what," he said. "Come back with your parents' and your grandmother's death certificates," Cook said steering them to the lobby. "I'll see what I can find out to tell you. Just so you know, once a witness is dead the protection is ended."

Johanna smiled and nodded. Leslie still looked bewildered. They got into Johanna's car and drove without speaking for the next minutes.

"What do we do now?" Leslie asked. "I'm feeling more like a non-person than ever."

They were in Friday traffic and cars on the Bay Bridge had come to a slow stop-and-go crawl.

"I have an idea. You said your parents died when you were nine," Johanna said, turning to face her. "That means they had to register you for school. They had to fill out forms."

"Yes, but won't the information be the same as my birth certificate—fake?"

Up ahead were flashing red lights. They were picking up speed past an unfortunate rear-ender.

"Maybe, but when your grandparents registered you for high school, they would have had to submit new paperwork. It might be interesting to see the comparison. They were going through a divorce. They might have been inconsistent. I once found an address from a school application that led to someone verifying an ancestor."

Leslie fell silent again.

"My grandparents who may not have been my real my grandparents you mean?"

"Did you stay in contact with your . . . grandfather, when your grandmother passed?"

Leslie chewed her bottom lip.

"He used to send a card on my birthdays. I got the last one when I turned twenty-one." Leslie scowled. "To be fair, I moved after I graduated. I . . . I never responded to him." She paused, then continued when Johanna didn't comment. "The divorce was contentious. I sided with my grandmother. She was always there for me."

"Did you keep any of the birthday cards from your grandfather?" Johanna asked. "I'd like to start there."

Johanna walked Leslie to her car when they got back to the office.

"Yeah, I think I still have them. Was he the crook?" Leslie said. "Or, do you think one of my parents, or maybe even both were criminals?"

"We may never know. They could have been just witnesses to a crime." Johanna shrugged. "The thing to remember is they took care to make sure you'd be okay."

Settling into the car, Leslie gave her a look that was indecipherable. "I'll go through my papers at home and locate the death certificates for my parents and grandmother and get them to you."

"And don't forget the birthday cards." Johanna said.

TRINIDAD

ALL MORNING TRINIDAD REPEATEDLY TRIED TO reach Maryanne Copeland, at least six times in three hours. She could hear Marty tapping away on the computer keyboard. She was about to click off after the seventh attempt when a voice responded.

"Yeah?"

"Hello, Mrs. Copeland, my name is Trinidad Owens," she said. "I am calling for your niece Simone Griffin. She—"

"You talk funny. Are you an American? Is Simone in trouble?"

"Sorry, mom, I try to speak clearer. Yes, I am an American citizen, and no Simone is not in trouble," Trinidad responded. "I am calling to ask that I come to see you?"

"You want to see me, why?"

Trinidad thought about her next words.

"There are some things that should be said in person. Simone has asked that I help her with—"

"With what now? She's always whining about something. I stopped taking her calls. Now she wants me to have foreigners . . . uh, aliens, in my own home."

"I am not an alien. I did not know she called you. But I do have something to tell you and to ask you."

"Ask me now, and I'll see if I can answer, and I'll see if I want to talk."

Trinidad was tired. It had already been a long day and she was ready to go home to a soak in the tub. This woman must be a test from the universe.

"Who is Simone's biological father?"

There was a long silence.

"Mrs. Copeland?"

"What does she know?"

"She has asked me to help discover answers. She is determined to find out," Trinidad replied. "And, I am starting with you. I do not like talking about these things on the phone. May I make a time to see you? Or, I can keep calling back until you are available."

"What nerve." Copeland snapped. "I'll only speak once. I'm busy this weekend. If you must, come on Monday, anything to have you stop bugging me," Copeland spat. "But, she's not coming with you, right?"

CHAPTER SEVEN

JOHANNA RETURNED FROM A RELATIVELY QUIET weekend ready to tackle return calls, review new correspondence, and start work on the Leslie Todd file. From the stack of death certificates and birthday cards in their envelopes now piled on top of the small table in her office, Johanna felt the surge of energy that came with a new client. Leslie had stuffed them in a plastic shopping bag and it was left at the reception desk.

"A woman said to give this to you. She was helping a friend by dropping it off and she was late for her spa treatment. Then she dashed out," Marty said, holding out the sack. "I'm sorry, I didn't get her name."

"No worries. I know what it is." Johanna smiled. "You can log the material as belonging to the Leslie Todd files."

"Got it." He wrinkled his brow. "You know, I've been thinking. How about I create a documents log for materials and any items clients might bring?" He pointed to the bag. "That way there's a separate file for paperwork and one for . . . ah, objects."

"You mean like in a police evidence room?" Johanna grinned.

He responded with a chuckle. "Yeah, except instead of a room, it will be an evidence file cabinet."

"Go for it."

Johanna thought for the umpteenth time what a great idea Marty was turning out to be. It was surprising how useful his ideas were over the last couple of days.

At her desk, she pulled from the near bottom of the bag, a pile what appeared to be unopened cards. All were postmarked, Sebastopol, California—no return address. She paused in thought. Sebastopol was a small northern California city in Sonoma County. In recent decades wine grapes had become the predominant agriculture crop, and nearly all lands once used for orchards were now vineyards. She glanced at a marketing mailer for an upcoming festival from the previous year. About 20 years ago the Sebastopol Documentary Film Festival became a big deal, rivaling the Sundance Film Festival, only the Sebastopol Festival focused on the environment and social justice. She had read somewhere the festival's entries could now qualify for an Academy Documentary Short Subject Award. She stared at one of the festival's listed donors.

Carl Luden.

Leslie's grandfather's name, that is if he was her grandfather, was Carl Luden. It was the name listed as parent on Leslie's mother's death certificate.

She picked up the first card. It was a birthday card dated eight years previous. It was signed simply: *Love Grandad*, in a blue Sharpie pen. She kept up sorting dates. Leslie was right, the last card was sent ten years ago. It was one of those cards that were blank on the inside. He had written a short note: *I've realized life is about family even if they're not your blood, and if they are . . . doesn't mean they're family. You know where to find me. Love Grandad.* It was written in the same blue Sharpie pen. Johanna had compared his name to an enclosed business card:

Life on a Vine
Bodega Highway Trail
Sebastopol, CA 95402
Proprietor: Carl Luden

She reached for her keyboard and Googled Carl Luden—nothing. Then she tried Life on a Vine—nothing. Then, Bodega Highway Trail—nothing. Undaunted, she queried the Sebastopol Chamber of Commerce and Visitors Center for Carl Luden—nothing. Now she was beginning to understand how Leslie felt during her search attempts.

She picked up her cellphone and punched in a number. It went to voicemail.

"Leslie, give me a call when you get this message."

Giving one last look at the business card, she returned it to the envelope and pulled out the flat white envelope containing the death certificates. Johanna looked over the names again.

Leslie's parents real names—maybe. Her grandparent's real names—maybe.

"What's up?" Ava looked over the top rim of her glasses at Johanna standing in her doorway. "I passed by your office earlier and judging by your desktop, you looked knee deep in research. However, now you appear to be somewhat discombobulated."

"If that means frustrated? I am." Johanna said, taking a deep sigh. "The Todd file is full of background—false background. I've never seen anything like it. I thought Leslie was just a novice at running information to ground, but I keep hitting walls, too. I'm not sure where to go next."

Johanna dropped into the chair in front of Ava's desk and took a swallow of water from the bottle she'd brought with her.

"I take it the death certificates weren't helpful," Ava said.

"If you mean the death certificates for Norman and Angela Todd—that would be correct. I had already checked with Sonoma County—the County that supposedly issued this certificate." She held it up. "The attending physician who signed the certificate is dead. Okay, so that's not really strange—people die." She leaned forward. "But then it gets really weird. I went a step further and, digging deep, it turns out he was dead four years before his signature was attached."

"You are kidding me. By the way, that's a terrible pun." Ava straightened. "Sounds like the U.S. Marshals don't mess around when they provide a new identity."

"Oh, it gets better," Johanna said. "Leslie told me she couldn't find any public records for her parents, so I was prepared for that, but look at this." She lifted out the business card supplied to Leslie by her grandfather. "Why would anyone have a calling card for a business that doesn't exist? This . . . this is to his own grandchild. He says she'll know where to find him. I doubt he really meant for her to locate him." She held the card out. "I have checked every utility, the chamber of commerce, the county's business license office, and several advertising outlets. Nada. And, Sebastopol isn't big."

"That's because it's not Sebastopol." Marty had entered, and he looked over her shoulder. "That's the zip code for Calistoga."

"What! Calistoga." Johanna turned to face him with an apprais-ing look. "Thanks, Marty."

Standing, she slipped past him and hurried to her office. When she tapped out the business and its correct phone number her screen scrolled several lines of text.

She murmured, "I got you, Carl Luden."

Johanna found herself shaking her head again and again. It was fortuitous Marty's last, and apparently only job required a mem-ory for zip codes to process client claims. A mind skill he clearly excelled in.

He passed by her office while she was waiting on hold. She whispered, "I owe you a donut."

Marty grinned and gave her a mock salute and headed back to the lobby.

She tapped in the number on her phone.

"Luden."

"Mr. Luden, my name is Johanna Hudson," she rushed, reach-ing for a pen. "I'm a genealogist and calling for benefit of your granddaughter Leslie Todd."

The silence was deafening.

"Mr. Luden?"

Finally.

"How did you get this number?"

"From the business card you sent Leslie. She asked me to help her uncover her background—find out about her parents' history."

"I don't know what your scheme is lady," he growled. "But you're not talking to my granddaughter, I don't have a granddaughter named Leslie."

He clicked off.

What the hell!

Johanna slammed her back into the chair. She picked up her phone and glanced at the time. Leslie had not returned her earlier call so she must be busy at work. Determined, Johanna began tapping again to find out what she could about Life on the Vine—with the correct zip code.

Nothing.

Fighting mounting aggravation when her phone pinged moments later, she grabbed it.

"Leslie, I've been trying to reach you," she rushed. "Sorry to leave so many messages but something has come up."

"I'm driving and just leaving the job," Leslie answered in an anxious voice. "I usually work from home but I went in today for a meeting. What is it?"

Johanna paused to take a slow breath.

"The business card you gave me for your grandfather, doesn't appear to be . . . to be valid." She paused. "I'm not even sure it was from your grandfather. The man who answered to the number on the card, said he didn't know a Leslie."

There was joyous laughter on the other end. Johanna was puzzled.

"What? What is it?"

"Oh, Johanna, you found him!"

"I did? But . . . but he didn't seem to know you."

"He doesn't know me, maybe at least not as Leslie. Johanna, I forgot. His nickname for me was Rosebud. You know like the sled in the movie?"

Johanna tilted in her head in puzzlement. "He named you after a sled? What movie?"

"Yes, yes it was a sled." Leslie's elation could be heard as she pounded on her steering wheel. "He loved 'Citizen Kane', you know the old 1940's movie with Orson Welles. He had a sled he loved named Rosebud." Her voice lowered and slowed. "Can I come to your office and we can call him together? No, wait. Wonder if you call him, give him my nickname, and he doesn't want to talk to me?" She mused. "I wasn't very nice to him. Assuming he knew it was me you were talking about, and he only pretended not to know."

Johanna mentally recounted the less-than-warm Luden conversation, and agreed. She let Leslie muse on the possibilities.

Johanna broke the quiet.

"You're right. Let me try calling him again with your nickname. That's probably what he meant in his card when he wrote you would know how to get in touch with him," she said. "I can bring him up to date with what's been happening with you. He probably thought I was a spammer or something."

Or something.

"Would you? I'd like you to be the intermediary for now just in case he's not ready for me. I don't know if I could handle the rejection," Leslie said. "Just try to get a day and time from him. I . . . I do want to see . . . meet him." She took a breath. "It doesn't matter when you set it up. I'll make myself available."

Johanna heard the wistful request in her client's voice.

"Sure, I'll call you as soon as I finalize things," she said.

Johanna's instincts told her it was unlikely Luden would pick up if he saw her number again so she used the office landline.

"Hello."

Johanna noticed he didn't use the business name.

"Mr. Luden, please don't hang up, it's Johanna Hudson again. I'm calling for Rosebud."

There was a long pause.

"Rosebud," he murmured.

"Yes, she wants to see you."

"Why?" he asked in a much stronger voice. "Why's she so anxious to see me after all these years? She made it clear she wanted nothing to do with me."

"Time has a way of highlighting what's important. She's trying to research her family—parents and . . . grandparents."

Johanna left it at that, there was no need to go into further detail until she knew he was willing to talk.

"I don't know. This is not a good time," he said. "It's complicated. I live a . . . a busy but private life and I like it that way."

"Leslie only wants a visit with you. I think she realizes there is so little she knows about her background. You're the only relative she knows that's left, unless, you can point her in another direction."

"Nah, there's no other direction. My daughter is gone," he said. "What's your name again? What business are you in?"

"My name is Johanna Hudson with Legacy Consultants. We do genealogy research—family trees. That's why Leslie contacted us," she paused then, "Mr. Luden, please consider seeing Leslie. It would mean so much and take up just a little of your time."

She could hear a series of deep breaths on the other end.

"I know I'm going to regret this. But, all right I'll meet with her. It's been years since I've seen her. I never thought I would see her again. It will be good to see how she has grown. She was a cute young lady like her mother," he said. "Make it this Thursday at six o'clock. I have a meeting at five. You got the address on the card, right?"

"Yes, it's a little vague though."

"Take the Old Bodega Highway Trail to the Parakeet Farm sign. Make a left across the road, and follow the driveway about two miles to the house." He stopped and took another deep breath. "Tell her . . . tell her it will be good to see her."

An hour later, even though on the phone Leslie's whoop of joy brought a smile to Johanna's lips.

"Before you get too excited, I'm not sure how much time he'll have for a visit. So we to think about what questions you have for him."

"But, he said he would be glad to see me, didn't he?"

"Yes, he did, but still we need to be prepared."

They took the next minutes to start on Leslie's list of questions. Johanna didn't know how much time they would have to discover answers, so the important questions had better be up front and ready.

"Think about any more you might have, and we'll talk." Johanna

"You know, I'm studying to be a museum docent," Leslie said. "I volunteer at a private collection. I'm surrounded by all this history and now I'm going to find out about my own.

I've . . ."

Johanna waited for her to continue.

"Yes?"

"I've wanted to know for so long and now I'm scared to find out."

TRINIDAD

THE DRIVE TO SAN JOSE HAD BEEN UNEVENTFUL and Trinidad took the time to run various scenarios through her head. She would sugar-talk Simone's aunt, Maryanne Copeland, into revealing, or at least providing a path, to her client's paternity. She located the condo without incident. It was actually on the border of Fremont, gratefully a city with plenty of on-street parking. Copeland had let her in without returning her greeting. Trinidad had taken the seat in front of the home's bay window next to an artificial fireplace with a faux dark wood acrylic mantel.

Now, only a few minutes later, Trinidad resisted the urge to look at her phone for the second time. There had been silence ever since she'd asked Maryanne Copeland the one question: who was Simone Griffin's biological father?

For her answer, Copeland, sat on the plastic-covered sofa, staring past her to look out the window—silent.

Maryanne Copeland was a large woman, overweight, and almost six feet tall. Her gray hair with streaks of brown was pulled into a tight braided bun, and the frown lines around her mouth were deep. Her gray eyes matched her hair and gave her an overall appearance of intimidation and reserve. An appearance, Trinidad had no doubt the woman cultivated. Her home smelled stale. It needed airing out. Trinidad also had no doubt Copeland could use fresh air herself, as well.

Trinidad cleared her throat.

"Mrs. Copeland, thank you so much for letting me interrupt your day. Simone is very anxious to find out about . . . about her birth father."

"I don't know who he is." She stood, and walked heavily toward the door. "Sorry you came out all this way."

Trinidad, her lips tightened as she tried to hide her surprise at the woman's rudeness, remained seated. "Ah, Mrs. Copeland I did hope you would be able to tell me who he is, but it will still be worth my effort, if you could tell me anything about Simone's father."

At her words, the woman appeared to drop her guard and peered at Trinidad until her eyes started to glisten. Returning to sit, her body appeared to sink in on itself. Blinking, she once more turned to stare out the window.

Hence the start of another silence.

After a couple of minutes more, Trinidad once more cleared her throat.

Copeland broke her stare and glanced down at her hands in her lap.

She scrutinized Trinidad. "Why do you wear so much black? Are you in mourning?"

"Wha . . . what do you mean?" Caught off guard, Trinidad did not bother hiding her irritation. "You have not seen me before."

"Are you?"

"No," Trinidad snapped, and then her voice shook. "Well, maybe . . . yes, my light has gone out. I lost a friend."

"So, did I. I lost my . . . my family."

Trinidad saw pain in the woman's face.

"What was Simone's mother like?"

Copeland rose to her feet.

"I guess you're not leaving. Want some coffee?"

To Trinidad it was revealing how much conversation could be had in silence. She followed Copeland into the spotless kitchen and took a seat on a bar stool along a linoleum-topped peninsula. The smell of household cleaner and bleach was intense, and the aroma of coffee was no match. Trinidad wrinkled her nose.

The pot needed only a button push. Coffee was poured. Remaining silent, Trinidad was half-way through the cup of coffee when Copeland spoke.

"I named her. Simone, I mean." She sipped looking past Trinidad. "Her mother, my sister Tanya, was no saint—we grew apart, for a lot of reasons but I loved her." Copeland brushed at a tear that had slipped through.

Trinidad handed her a paper napkin. "I am sorry about your sister."

Copeland shrugged, dabbing at her eyes. "I have to say this, Tanya may have had her issues, but she was a good mother to Simone. That little girl cried night and day for five years growing up, and then advanced to whining. Tanya was the only one able to get her quiet—even laughing sometimes." Her voice drifted in memory.

Trinidad was tempted to take notes. The contradictory picture of Simone's mother, and Simone, did not match. But, she was afraid with any interruption Maryanne Copeland would stop recalling.

"And her father?"

"What?" Copeland gave a small shake of her head bringing her back. "Oh, I . . . I don't want to talk about him. He was already married. Tanya was . . . well she was spoiled she wanted what she wanted. When she found out she was pregnant, she grabbed onto Phil Griffin who married her and was a good husband and a true father. They didn't have children together." Copeland abruptly stopped and peered at Trinidad. "I'm telling you all this for Simone. I won't repeat it, so you don't have to bring Simone to see me. She'll remind me of too many bad memories. I told you all I know, now you can tell her."

"But Maryanne—may I call you Maryanne?"

"No." The woman snapped and fiercely stirred her cooling coffee.

"All right then, Ms. Copeland, I will tell you Simone is dying." Trinidad paused when she saw Copeland's eyes widening. "She has good memories of you. She wanted to tell you herself, but it appears that is not to be. She hoped you could help her locate her birth father."

"No, I can't. I don't know where he is." Copeland put her hand to her forehead and said, "It's not like you think. I can't help you." She took a deep breath. "Tanya had the same condition. It's the iron, right? How long does Simone have?"

Trinidad took the next minutes to explain Simone's disease and progression. "The doctors told her six months, maybe a year."

"Six months." She repeated, shaking her head again. Averting her eyes, she changed the subject. "You know, you're not a bad person—for a foreigner. You wear your black on the outside and I wear mine on the inside." She frowned and looked over her shoulder at the refrigerator covered in notes and pictures. "Simone . . . Simone like I said, brings up bad memories for me. Look, my sister might have your answers. I don't have them in me. Phil always had a crush on Tanya. He married her, but no, he was not Simone's birth father. Anyway, Tanya stopped talking to me."

"Simone has another aunt?"

"Yep, there were three of us. Me, Audrey and Tanya. My sister Audrey wasn't an angel either, none of us are . . . were," Copeland said matter of fact. "I'm the black sheep of the family. I haven't spoken to any of them in six years, right after Tanya passed. Before then we hadn't spoken in . . ." She squinted in recollection. ". . . In almost 20 years."

"*Oveja negra*—black sheep. Oh my, what did you do?"

Copeland gave a hearty laugh. "Now, why would I tell you?"

CHAPTER EIGHT

The ride to Napa Valley consisted mostly of Leslie recounting tales of what she knew from her childhood, her parents and then life with her grandparents. She wanted to drive and Johanna was glad to focus on listening. She didn't want to interrupt the flow of remembrances might be lead to unrecognized critical information.

"Here I am a grown woman, hoping for a family of my own, coming to grips with the fact that my entire life . . . my background was a fraud," Leslie said with only a hint of regret. "I don't know what I will find out from my grandfather, but it will go a long way to filling in my history."

"I can only imagine," Johanna murmured.

"No, you can't. I don't say that in a mean way, but you can't possibly know what it feels like to be suspended in mid-air forever. In the Middle East there is a saying: I feel like a bird without a branch to land on," Leslie's voice choked. "That's me. I—"

Johanna's phone pinged. She glanced down. It was Ava. She tapped a quick 'get back to you' response, and returned her eyes to the road.

Leslie sounded wistful. "I guess I just want to land."

The Parakeet Farm sign was where Luden had said, but the road across the highway was little more than a narrow unpaved single lane. Leslie's car mowed through the padded dried brush and clusters of dandelions. There was no house or structure in sight. She kept driving.

"Johanna, don't get discouraged, this looks like we're going down the road he described."

"I'm glad you're feeling confident," she murmured. Then trying to show more certainty she added, "You're right, your grandfather did say we would have to drive a little ways."

Finally, the roof top of a house appeared in slope of the hillside. Johanna took a breath of relief. Then she frowned.

There were two cars parked in front of a small ranch style house.

"Looks like Grandad has a visitor."

"Yes," Johanna said, getting a wary feeling in her gut.

They parked in a patch of high weeds to the side of the vehicles. Far from the highway traffic, there was complete silence. Opening the car door, Leslie looked apprehensively at Johanna. She got out of the car, but stayed close to the vehicle.

"You go first," Leslie said. "I'll need just a moment."

Johanna gave her an encouraging smile and made her way to the front door and knocked. There was no answer. She knocked harder.

"Mr. Luden," she called out. "It's Johanna Hudson and Leslie, er . . . Rosebud."

Silence engulfed the house. The windows were shuttered. She would have to go around the back.

"Leslie, get back inside the car and wait until I can reach your grandfather. Maybe he can't hear us." Johanna gave a gentle wave. "I'll go to the back and see if I can rouse him."

Leslie nodded without speaking, but did not move to get out of the car.

Showing much more bravado than she was feeling, Johanna walked gingerly alongside the house, which was more like a large shed. The weeds were almost to her hip. She'd worn sneakers but no socks, and the stickers from the thorny thistle were slipping into the sides of her shoes and driving her crazy. Because the house was on a slope and the placement of the windows were higher than she could see into. As she made her path along side, she could see it wasn't a big house but had what appeared to be a crude stucco addition extending out into another stretch of land.

She came to the end of the structure.

There were three steps leading up to a small porch that held battered sliding glass doors. Johanna instinctively steeled her nerves. Her heartbeat was rapid and her breath came in short intakes.

One of the glass doors was open several inches.

"Mr. Luden," she raised her voice leaning in. "Mr. Luden, it's Johanna—"

At first, she didn't see the body lying in the shade of the hallway between the apparent kitchen and the rest of the house. Squinting, the shadow took form. Then, her eyes were unable to pull away from the figure curled in a fetal position. Sliding the door fully open, she entered the dark room and cautiously edged forward.

"Mr. Luden, are you okay?" She bent down to touch his shoulder. "I came with—"

Then she saw the pool of blood oozing from the head. She heard herself scream. There was a distant scuffle, and then everything went dark.

CHAPTER NINE

J OHANNA'S EYES FLITTED OPEN, THEN QUICKLY narrowed at the pinpoint beam of light.

"Can you hear me Mrs. Hudson?"

She started to nod, but a sharp pain crossed her forehead. "Yes," she whispered.

"Good. I'm Randy Francis. I'm an EMT. You're in an ambulance." He enunciated each word. "We're taking you to Claremont Hospital."

"Hospital. What happened to me?"

"Johanna, I followed you," Leslie, sitting next to her gurney, loudly whispered. "When I came in the back door, you were on the floor and Phillip . . . the body next to you was . . ." She shivered. "I called 9-1-1."

"We're going to want to speak with you both," a female uniformed officer said. "We'll have someone meet you at the hospital."

Johanna's eyes searched for understanding in those of the young red-haired attendant holding an oxygen mask. He took it away when she spoke.

"I think . . . I was . . . there was . . . yes I saw the body, and . . ."

"Sh, just stay quiet for now. You had a blow to the head, but you appear to be all in one piece. The police are following us to the emergency room and they'll talk to you there—if you're up to it."

"Up to it . . . a blow to the head?" she repeated, and then added, "Carl Luden, is he dead?

"Oh, Johanna, I don't know what happened at that house," Leslie said. "But I know the man on the floor."

JOHANNA MUST HAVE DOZED OFF, but it wasn't a sound sleep, the beeping of a device and a distant intercom on a seemingly continuous loop invaded her mental space. The antiseptic smell caused her to wrinkle her nose. She turned her head slightly and opened one eye.

He was still sitting there. She'd noticed him earlier when she woke the first time.

"Officer?"

"No, I'm a detective, Mrs. Hudson. My name is Detective Daniel Ward," he said as he stood slipping the cell phone he'd been scrolling into a shirt pocket. "I know this is a bad time for you, but I'm hoping you can give us something to go on, to help us find who attacked you and who killed Phillip Nava."

She blinked several times. "Phillip Nava?" Her vision was clearing. "I was there to see Carl Luden. I . . . I don't know a Phillip Nava."

"Carl Luden? Who is he?" He tilted his head in scrutiny, reaching for his phone and hitting the audio. "Mrs. Hudson, can you take me through what you did tonight and what you were doing at Nava's house?"

Johanna tensed. *What happened? Who was Phillip Nava?*

"You said, tonight," she replied. "What time is it?"

He glanced at the time on one of her monitors. "It's close to nine p.m. on Thursday."

"Nine p.m.," she repeated. She'd lost hours. "My family, my business, they—"

"They know you're here. They're on their way. It was because they reported you missing to our local sheriff's office that we were able to ID you." He crossed his arms. "Your phone was gone but your car registration was in your glove compartment. We found your purse later."

She groaned—all her contacts.

"How did you find Nava?" He returned to sitting. "A woman told us you were meeting her grandfather. That he had directed you there. But she had never spoken with him—only you. Now we can't locate her. Who is she? How does Phillip Nava fit in?" he said, moving in closer to the side of the bed. "Just take it slow from the beginning."

Johanna explained about Legacy Consultants.

"I told Leslie—wait, where is she? She said she knew the man . . . Nava?"

"That's just it. We don't know where she is. What's her full name?" Ward soothed, as he scribbled down Johanna's response. "She didn't tell the EMS why you were meeting with Nava. She said she was only counting on seeing her grandfather."

"So was I," Johanna said, her head clearing. "Leslie Todd, is a new client. I was helping her find her grandfather, Carl Luden— not Phillip Nava. I don't know a Phillip Nava—period. We were there to meet Luden. He told us to meet him there."

"So you think Luden enticed his granddaughter, who he hadn't seen in years, to a meeting where she could be implicated in a murder?"

"No," Johanna shook her head. "That doesn't make any sense, even to me."

He scribbled a note on his small pad. "The woman . . . er, Leslie Todd told the medical technician, that she discovered you alone at the feet of the victim, Phillip Nava," he said. "Since she didn't know where you were going, she couldn't have known Nava would be there." He paused then continued. "Were you aware Nava has dark money connections? He has a criminal record."

"No, I was not aware. I told you I don't know a Phillip Nava. Have you found Carl Luden? It was his house."

"Actually, the house is owned by a family on the east coast who inherited it from their uncle. It hasn't been lived in for years. They are holding on to it waiting for land prices to rise. They do not know a Carl Luden."

"I guess I didn't verify the property deed. But we had out-reached to him."

"You had a little head injury; maybe you're getting things mixed up."

"What—"

Before she could finish her sentence, the door opened and Ava and Trinidad hurried to her bedside. Ward moved back to the wall.

"Johanna, oh my God. We were so worried." Ava picked up her hand, grasping it in hers. "Marty remembered the address, but GPS didn't know how to find it." Tears began to flow. "He was kicking himself for not having set up a file for Leslie Todd."

"I know you, Johanna," Trinidad said from the other side of the bed holding her other hand. "But I too was worried. I . . . I can't lose another friend. Good, your head only has a small bandage. What does the doctor say?"

The door whooshed open.

"The doctor says there are too many people in this room." She reached out her hand. "I'm Doctor Karen Davis." A woman wearing a white jacket and carrying an iPad entered. "Leave, all of you. She'll likely go home today, but I need to check her out. A nurse will meet you in the waiting area."

"Doctor, I'm Detective Ward with the sheriff's office, we—"

"Good to meet you, Detective, and now goodbye." She didn't look up from the device screen. "If you don't leave now, I'll testify anything she said to you today is suspect—she's had a head injury Detective."

Ward started to protest, but the withering glance from the physician was a warning he decided to take. He turned to Johanna. "I'll be in contact in the morning. I hope you're feeling better." He closed the door behind him.

Ava and Trinidad let Johanna's hands go with final squeezes.

Ava adjusted her purse on her shoulder. "Doctor, I'll be taking Johanna home with me. What time will she be released?"

"Depends, check in with the nurse's station."

Johanna understood the caution in the doctor's choice of words. She moistened her lips and raised her voice, "Ava, Luden disappeared. We never saw him. This guy Phillip Nava was there when they found me."

"This Nava person knows Leslie? How can that be, Johanna?" Trinidad frowned.

"I have my suspicions," she said. "And Luden wasn't there how—"

"What am I, a stalk of celery?" the doctor interjected. "Didn't I just ask you to leave? Go. Your being here is not helping her." She held her arms wide to herd them out.

CHAPTER TEN

"**Y**OU CAN STOP WHISPERING. THE OFFICE walls are thin, I can hear you," Johanna said her fingers tapping on the keyboard keys.

Her door opened. Ava and Trinidad entered, both with arms across their chests.

"Johanna, what are you doing here?" Trinidad said. "You should be home resting. We do not need you here—well, we do not need you here right now."

Ava took a step forward. "Trinidad is right. I know you want to find Leslie. We do too. But you're not going to find her if you can't think straight." She sat in the chair in front of the desk. "Look, tell us what happened. Let us help you, we can be your feet."

Johanna looked at both of her friends with gratitude.

"You are gems, but really I'm fine," she said. "The sedative they gave me made me loopy, but the little pain I had is gone. I had a good sleep last night. I needed to come in. I'm more frustrated and . . . and worried more than anything." Johanna took a breath. "And, yes it would be great to have your help. I have a feeling we don't have much time."

"Good, we will help you." Trinidad took the remaining chair. "I agree with Ava we have your feet. Now, take us through everything that happened on Saturday."

After a quick moment of puzzlement, Johanna and Ava exchanged a smile and look of translation understanding.

During the next half-hour Johanna brought them up-to-date with her client's file and the happenings on the murderous day. Both Trinidad and Ava had reached for nearby writing pads to take notes.

"I can't believe it was just yesterday." Johanna shook her head. "The police interviewed me before I left the hospital and said they would be in touch. But nothing so far today. I can't get a hold of Leslie. She's not returning my calls or texts." She ran her hands through her hair. "It's making me crazy. They can't find her. I can't find her. She's not picking up her cell."

"What does she look like?" Trinidad asked, pen poised.

Johanna had a thoughtful look. "You never saw her?"

Trinidad shook her head.

"I wouldn't recognize her either," Ava added.

Johanna sighed. "You're right we never met in the office. Marty met her when she dropped off her papers. Wait . . . no, he said a woman dropped them off for Leslie. I guess, he never met her either."

The three of them looked at each other.

"No, no . . . no, I know what you're thinking." Johanna shook her head. "Wait, Leslie and I met with this guy at the US Marshals office. He saw her with me. We didn't meet for a long time—he had to go to a meeting. But we did meet."

"Well, that's something," Ava said. "You're not completely bonkers."

Johanna rolled her eyes.

"No, I'm not losing my mind, but I have to wonder if there is a reason for her keeping a low profile.

AVA

"AVA, WHAT DO YOU MEAN YOU'RE THINKING about postponing your trip?" Eric leaned over the lunch table, his voice raised drawing the glances of diners at nearby tables. "You have to it's . . . it's a chance of a lifetime. This is a position you've always wanted. Are you just going to walk away from your dream?"

"Calm down," Ava said putting her hand out. "It's my dream not yours."

Eric stared at her, then nodded and lowered his voice. "Okay, that's true. I guess I was also thinking about Aunt Lillian. I spoke with Mom this morning making final arrangements for someone to meet you at the airport to get the package from you. It's really lousy timing. I guess I'll just have to call Mom back."

"Don't try to guilt me, Eric. If you feel so bad about the package, you take it to Aunt Lillian. You're the one who was originally supposed to go. But, I can't leave Legacy now. I'm going to check to see if I can join the dig in later in the fall. I don't have to be there at the very beginning."

She hoped the disappointment she felt didn't show. A major draw of the dig's adventure was the enticement to be there for the site planning at the beginning.

"Okay," he said. "Okay, let's start over. I know you're worried about Johanna, but at least it sounds like she's on her way back to recovery. Right? So, that worry is going to resolve itself." He grasped her hand. "I know we missed the mark as a couple, but let me help you with this. As a parting gift let me help you bring your life's goal to fruition."

"Eric, we parted over three years ago," Ava snapped.

"It seems like only yesterday," he replied with an exaggerated puppy dog look.

At that, they both laughed.

Silence came over the table as a server took their nods to pour refills of coffee. Ava put her hands around the cup to warm and inhaled the aroma. Eric waved the server away.

She took a sip and gazed out the window. "Why don't you tell me what's going on with you? Why all of a sudden are you trying to be the thoughtful ex-husband and the dutiful son—it's a questionable fit." She turned back to look into his eyes—the eyes that once could make her forget her name.

Eric gave her a lopsided smile. "Do you remember Kevin Gault? He used to come over when we lived on Warren Street. Real tall, spoke with a twang—he was a couple of years younger than me."

"Vaguely," Ava said. "Didn't he have a parrot?"

"Yes! That's him, I forgot about the parrot." Eric shook his head in memory. "Anyway, I went to his funeral a couple of days ago—"

"Eric, I'm sorry."

He shrugged. "He'd been ill for a while. But, my point is, there was hardly anyone there, Ava, just two people from his family in the room." He clasped his hands. "I don't want my . . . my last room to be empty. I'm trying to get my act together."

She raised her eyebrows at the glistening of tears forming, and took a deep breath.

"Alright, let me think on things," Ava said, dabbing her mouth with a napkin. She looked down at her Fitbit. "I've got to go. I'm not sure how you can help Legacy but I'll ask Johanna and Trinidad. We've got a couple of gnarly cases going and if I were to leave it would have to be when—"

"Doesn't matter. Give me a chance, that's all I ask."

"Ava, I hear what you are saying, but it is not me," Trinidad said as she tapped on her keyboard without looking up. "Johanna is the one who will think you are crazy."

"Where is she?"

"Public records, I tell her I can go but she wanted to search for herself because she doesn't know what she's looking for."

Trinidad squinted at the computer screen.

"What are you working on?" Ava came around the desk to look over Trinidad's shoulder. "Still trying to find Simone Copeland's father?"

"Yes, eventually. Right now I'm looking for Simone's aunt." Trinidad hit the keyboard. "And I found her."

The lunch with Eric had taken longer than she expected. Ava glanced at the time on her phone. The music loop on hold was in its fourth iteration and she was tempted to email Homeland Security with the suggestion they use this gimmick as a psychological tactic to breakdown the mental defenses of criminals.

Before she left to do research, Trinidad had suggested she call another number in the system.

"Ava, call another number on the department's contact list, and ask to be transferred," Trinidad offered. "I would like to stay and hear how this ends, but I must go. Marty you can call me if you need me, yes?"

He nodded.

As far as Ava was concerned, the new number hadn't worked and the hold music wasn't nearly as nice.

"Are you still on hold?" Marty asked from her office doorway. He motioned at her nod. "There's a man in the lobby—he's a little well, intense. He wants to see Johanna."

"Tell him she's not here and not expected back today. And tell him we don't take drop-ins." Ava didn't try to hide the irritation in her voice. "He should've made an appointment."

Marty nodded and turned to leave. Ava held up her hand.

"Wait, don't say those things." She clicked the phone off. "That's not good client service. I'll speak to him. I can spend all day tomorrow trying to get through to the insurance company."

"One other thing, he's a little . . . overbearing," Marty said. "He wouldn't give me his name. Just said Johanna knew him."

Ava pursed her lips. "Hmm, okay, let's go meet this mysterious stranger."

When she looked into the eyes of an elderly man standing next to the chair in the lobby Ava knew why Marty described him the way he did. Dressed simply in a blue uniform jacket with some sort of emblem, covering a pale blue shirt and tan Dockers. His piercing dark eyes didn't match the otherwise benign appearance.

He did not return her smile.

"Hello, I'm Ava Lowell. I'm Johanna Hudson's partner." She let her untouched hand drop to her side. "Can I help you?"

"I need to see Hudson. When will she be back?" His voice was low almost menacing.

Out of the corner of her eye, Ava caught Marty's slow, but steady movement inching toward the back of his desk. She didn't want to think about what he was up to.

Evidently the stranger saw him, too.

"What are you getting ready to do?" He called out to Marty.

"Me?" Marty put his hand to his chest and with his best innocent look. "Nothing, I was just going back to my work."

"Look, sir," Ava said exasperated. "It's been a long day. What is your name? Johanna will get in touch with you when she returns. However, I don't expect her back until tomorrow—"

Just then the lobby door opened and Johanna entered.

"Hey, everybody I—" She stopped when she saw the gathering. "Hello," she nodded to the man, and then sent a questioning look to Ava. "Hi Ava, is this a new client of yours?"

"No." Ava gave her a pointed smile. "He's looking for you. I was just getting his name."

Johanna took a step back and Marty took a step forward.

"Sorry." He ran his hand over his head. "Yes, I know she was looking for me." He paused and then began again this time his voice was lower and controlled. "I didn't mean to frighten you earlier . . . any of you." He looked at each of them. "But it's important I know."

"Know what? Who are you?" Johanna asked, seemingly more curious than fearful.

"I'm Carl Luden. I understand you want to talk to me."

CHAPTER ELEVEN

"**W**HERE'S LESLIE?" JOHANNA BLURTED, when they were behind the closed doors of her office.

"Don't you know where she is?" Luden said. "I had to leave the house before you got there. It wasn't safe. There was . . . well you know."

"You left us there!" Johanna shouted. "We could have been killed. I was attacked. Leslie found what she thought were two bodies and called 9-1-1. She was scared to death. Didn't you see her?"

"From a distance, yes. But it couldn't be helped," he said. "Something came up. I'm working with the government and I can't be seen. I knew the police were on their way."

"Working with the government, really?" Johanna said. "I guess you didn't notice the bodies in your kitchen you had to step over when you headed for the front door?"

"I don't know Nava's body was going to be there," Luden insisted. "I know what you're thinking, but I didn't kill him. "What do the police say? The newspapers are sketchy."

"The police don't confide in me, but they are looking for you." Johanna said. "And Leslie, Leslie was totally distraught. She's not returning my calls. She thought she was going to reunite with her grandfather and instead she's party to a crime scene. That's a bit much for anyone."

"Look, there was a lot of confusion." Luden's eyes narrowed and his back straightened. "I had completely planned on meeting my granddaughter and getting back in touch with her life. I wanted us to be part of a family again. She has not had it easy." He gave her a sad smile.

Johanna blinked, she had caught the thin lines of pulled facial skin—Luden was wearing a disguise.

"Mr. Luden, I don't want to make things harder on Leslie. I felt sorry for her. My only involvement was to help her connect with you," Johanna said. "She asked me to help her reunite with her family—that's all."

"Didn't she give you her information?

"Yes, but like I said, she's not responding to my contacts," Johanna said. "I didn't know Philip Nava at all, and still don't," Johanna said. "The police told me his name because I found his body when I came to your house—with Leslie. I was hit on the head, and when I came to, Leslie was standing over me in an ambulance, and you were nowhere around."

Luden just stared into space. "I'm going to need your help. I'll pay your fee."

"All right, but if you want me to assist you I'm going to need to need real information. Let's start from the beginning," Johanna said. "To be upfront, like I said, I haven't been able to reach Leslie since that night either."

"They might have her." Luden murmured.

Johanna stiffened.

"Who are *they*?"

The question startled Luden out of his trance. "I can't tell you, and believe me you wouldn't want me too. What do you think you know?"

Johanna straightened in her chair.

"I know you, or someone in your family, is in the US Marshal's Witness Protection Program. Is that the government you're working for? Then I would say it was you in the program." Johanna searched his eyes for acknowledgement. "I know your wife and children died while living a life paying for your wrongdoing. And, I know another generation—your own granddaughter is still paying. And . . . and I know you just killed a man."

Luden's eyes narrowed and Johanna clamped her shaking arm next to her body.

"I didn't kill anyone."

Johanna felt she wasn't in a position to argue the facts with him, but she first had to know what happened to her young client.

"Where would *they* take Leslie?" she asked. "If *they* did have her."

Luden frowned.

"I had some ideas, but she's not there," he said. "I haven't seen her since she was a young adult. Since I . . . I had to . . . withdraw. My daughter, Angie—Angela, left home after college and only rarely visited me. With our new life, my wife and I were always looking over our shoulders. My daughter, brought Leslie with her only a couple of times to visit. Then Donna and I got divorced. Leslie was just a teenager the last time I saw her."

He shook his head and pointed to Johanna as if in accusation.

"How did you meet her?"

Johanna leaned back in her chair, and quickly summarized Leslie's search for her true background and her outreach to Legacy.

Luden, looked at his watch and turned toward the door.

"Look," he said. "Things are up in the air right now. How did Leslie know to get in touch with *you*?"

"There was an article in the paper about our service," Johanna said. "She came to me because she was feeling lost and confused. "Everything she thought she knew about her past has dissolved. She wants to find the only person in her life, her grandfather, who knows her full story—her real story."

He took another look at his watch.

"Please, just give me five more minutes. I'm still trying to digest all this," Johanna said, creasing her brow and leaning over the table.

"When we went to meet you at the house in Napa, did you see us pull up? Did you see the woman with me?"

"Yes, and no. About an hour before we were to meet I staked myself out at the Parakeet Farm—you know where you have to turn left to get to my place. It's good as a lookout. I haven't lived this long taking people at their word. I needed to make sure you were legit."

Johanna nodded in understanding.

"A grey SUV turned onto the road, but it wasn't two women. It was a man."

"Philip Nava?" Ava asked.

"Yeah, Nava."

"So, you're saying you got away," Johanna said. "You never saw us arrive?"

"No, I never saw you. I turned around and drove over to San Raphael, where I have a place I can stay. I thought I might have dodged a trap you set for me." Luden gave her a tight lipped smile.

"I set a trap for you. How could I? I didn't know where I was going."

"Maybe." He shrugged. "It wasn't until I read the paper the next morning that I knew the full story of what happened. And it wasn't until yesterday's news, when I saw your name on the screen that I found out about what happened to you."

Johanna wasn't sure she believed him. They had come to a point of mutual distrust.

"Still, there are too many coincidences," Johanna slowly shook her head.

"Look, the one thing this debacle has made clear is my family did nothing to deserve the life of lies I surrounded them in." Frowning, he turned to Johanna. "I've been thinking about this, I want you to bring my granddaughter to meet with me. Tell her, I can talk to her about her past, her ancestors, family history—anything she wants. I'm going away soon. I won't be able to stay in touch."

"Why not?" Johanna persisted. "And don't forget the body in your house. What about Phillip Nava? Who is he? Who killed him?" She persisted.

"I don't know," he said. "I've never killed anyone in my life. Nava is . . . was a piece of work. The world is a safer place with him gone."

She noticed he didn't answer all her questions.

"Who wanted him dead?"

His eyes narrowed. "Too many choices."

"Well, the police are looking for you. I'm sorry, I told them everything I could," she said.

Luden seemed to look through her.

"Listen, I can't be here any longer. I don't stay any place too long. You can see what happens when I do. I'll contact you in a couple of days. Find Leslie."

Standing, he paused at the door turning to look back at her.

"I may be wrong to trust you, but I've been wrong before."

"Wait," Johanna said, realizing she had already accepted the hunt. "Give me something to get started on. The protection program didn't seem to have anything on Leslie. Which reminds me, what about the protection program? Do they know about your escape . . . your role in the Napa murder?" Johanna asked.

"Nah, they know nothing." He pushed his chest out. "Todd, was her father's family name. They lived in Healdsburg. Try looking for a Leslie Summers that was the name we used to raise our daughter—Leslie's mother. It makes me glad Leslie even remembers me." He gave Johanna a small smile. "I'm the one who gave her the nickname, Rosebud. Only her mother knew of the name." Luden took out his wallet and handed over a folded picture. "This is my daughter."

Johanna stared at the picture of the beaming young woman with her arm around her father, a young Luden. She wore her dark hair in a pixie cut and dark brown eyes that teased impishness. His face was in shadow.

"We're not supposed to keep old snapshots. But I couldn't wipe everyone out." he said grimly taking back the photo. "By the way, the name Carl Luden is a pick up name. In case you're thinking of telling the police. I never entered the federal witness protection program, well I did, but I didn't stay. I changed my name to Luden when I left. The feds know the name, but not the face. I couldn't take the chance, too many leaks. If I had stayed, I'd be dead by now."

TRINIDAD

WALKING UP THE DIRT FOOT PATH to Audrey Copeland's house, Trinidad swatted at a fly that seemed to have adopted her as a potential friend. Then his brother whizzed by her head. Annoyed she looked around for a source of the gathering insects, and spotted a nearby pile of pungent dog droppings centimeters from the entry. Wrinkling her nose, she sidestepped the mound and knocked on the front door. There was no doorbell.

There was no response.

She readied to knock a little firmer but before she could, the door opened—six inches.

"Yes?"

The woman who answered was too young to be Simone's aunt. Her horn-rimmed glasses caught the glare from the sun. Trinidad cleared her throat.

"Hello, I am Trinidad Owens. I am with Legacy Consultants we do genealogy charts. Is Mrs. Wallace available to speak with me? I would like to talk to her about her sister, Tanya."

"She doesn't —"

The door snatched open and the smell of cabbage wafted into the doorway.

"Maryanne called. First time in, I don't know how many years to tell me about you. I hung up on her. My sister, Tanya is dead, Miss Owens," said the elderly woman in a pink metal wheelchair wearing a frizzy red wig slightly off center. "We buried her years ago. What do you want?"

"Your sister, Maryanne, said you might help me. I—"

"That bitch. You're not carrying a gun are you?"

"No, I do not—"

"Knife?"

"No, I—"

"Then what do you want?"

Trinidad, with one eye on the dog leavings, swatted at a fly and crossed her arms over her chest.

"If you let me speak, I want to come inside and talk to you about your niece, Simone. She needs you." She motioned with her head toward the entry. "Please."

There was a silence.

"Tanya's daughter? You gotta' card?"

Trinidad nodded. Reaching into her briefcase she pulled out a Legacy card and handed it over.

"Oh, all right then," The woman said, rolling back a few inches and gestured to the younger woman to allow her inside. "Come in. You're from the islands aren't you?" She went on after Trinidad's nod, "I went to Barbados a long time ago on a cruise."

"I am from Trinidad-Tobago." Trinidad smiled.

"Never heard of it." She rolled her chair in front of a small red brick fireplace barely missing Trinidad's feet. "I'm sorry for my harsh tone. It's just my sister, and I use the term *sister* in the narrow sense— we stopped speaking many years ago. What is it you do again?"

Trinidad took account of a woman likely in her late sixties maybe early seventies with heavily wrinkled skin and a cataract in her right eye. She was wearing a moss green jogging suit.

"Mrs. Copeland, I—"

"Call me, Audrey. And, this is Jane," she said pointing. "She takes care of me, with cooking and things. In fact, Jane why don't you go on back to the kitchen and finish making lunch. I'm getting hungry and I'll eat before you go home." She waved her off.

Jane, still not saying a word, tilted her head in acknowledge-ment to Trinidad, and left the room.

"I don't get many visitors," Audrey said, her arms pushing on the chair's wheels. "You're very pretty." She squinted. "Nope, I don't get many guests, pretty or otherwise. Now, go ahead and tell me. What do you want again?"

"Call me, Trinidad," she hurried. "Audrey, like I said. I am here for Simone, Tanya's daughter. My company helps clients find their ancestors . . . and relatives from their background so they can pull together their family history." Trinidad moistened her lips. "Simone came to us wanting to find her father." She paused when the woman gasped. "I know, it has been a long time for her not to know, but Simone is sick."

"Sick, what's wrong with her?"

"She has a genetic disorder that attacks her liver." Trinidad sighed. "The doctors did not find it early, but there is still a chance they can turn it around."

"Is it that Chromatosis thing?" Audrey offered, rubbing her forehead.

"Yes," Trinidad said. "How did you know?"

"Because, Tanya had it. It's why she died."

"Well then, Audrey, that explains why I am here." Trinidad looked down at her hands. "To have the sickness, Simone must have two parents with the disease, but the man she knew as her father did not have this gene. So—"

"So, Simone knows Phil wasn't her father." Audrey rolled her chair across the room to a bookcase, again barely missing Trinidad's feet.

Trinidad tried to tuck them under the chair.

"Yes, I am afraid to say."

The bookcase was about four feet high, and jammed with as many magazines as books. Audrey bent down and with certainty pulled out a picture album. She flipped through until she found what she was looking for—and pressed the open page it to her chest.

"How will knowing her father help?"

"I think she is looking for answers." Trinidad shrugged. "She is looking for her family—her real identity."

Audrey sadly shook her head and held the album out to Trinidad.

"Look at the two couples under the awning, the blonde, that's Tanya. And Phil is next to her. He was her husband back then. That's my ex and me." She pointed with an arthritic finger to the other male. "He was cheat and a liar, he was just her type."

"I see."

"No, you probably don't. And I'm not going to open my family to your nosiness." She backed up her chair to the heating unit set inside the faux fireplace. "My sister Maryanne and Tanya were close. I know what she says, Maryanne doesn't want to admit caring for anyone. But she cared for Tanya. She pushed Tanya to marry Phil. Tanya was much younger than Maryanne and I. Still, no matter what Maryanne says what happened could be seen coming a mile away. Tanya was a slut, but a loveable slut. I wasn't able to have children," she paused, and continued, "but I treated Tanya like she was my own, until the end."

Trinidad shook her head thoroughly confused.

"It was good she had you."

Audrey gave her a faint smile.

"Yes, at least for a while." Her eyes glistened with unshed tears. She blinked them back. "But in the end it didn't matter. They were destroyers."

"What happened?" Trinidad asked softly.

"What happened? He happened." She swiped at her tears and quickly rolled her chair closer to the fireplace missing Trinidad's foot by a hair. "I don't know why I'm telling you all these things," she said clearly annoyed. "I hardly know you, I—"

Jane came into the room.

"Audrey, lunch is ready if you are."

The old woman frowned.

"Can you stay for lunch?" Audrey asked, her eyes pleading please.

"I am sorry," Trinidad responded. "But I must go back to my office to research the information you gave me."

She almost missed the crestfallen look on Audrey's face, which disappeared as quickly as it had appeared.

"No matter, I was just being polite. Jane and I will be fine." She abruptly whirled her chair toward the hallway.

Trinidad came around to stand in front of the elderly woman, blocking her advancement.

"Audrey, what I want to say is, please, I would like to have lunch with you, but another time." Trinidad placed her hand on top of the elderly woman's grip on the chair's arm rest. "If, all right? I would like to come back and bring Simone with me."

Audrey caught her breath and stared into Trinidad's eyes. Her grip relaxed.

"Oh yes, yes that would be very nice," Audrey said. "I haven't seen Simone since she was a baby." She shifted and looked troubled. "When would you come?"

"How about I call Jane tomorrow?" Trinidad said to Jane's nod. "I will have a chance to speak with Simone and I will know the best date."

"It doesn't matter what date," Audrey said moving back into the room. "I'm here all the time and I don't go anywhere."

"Very well, I will go now." Trinidad said, moving to the front door. "But, I will be back."

"With Simone?" Audrey rolled forward, just grazing the back of her heel.

Trinidad smiled.

At least she hoped so.

AVA

AVA TOOK ADVANTAGE OF THE OPEN SEATING in the park. The only other people there were a small energetic toddler chasing a fleeing cocker spaniel who was tugging on the leash held by its patient owner.

She paused and looked out toward the bay. The City of Alameda's coast view of the San Francisco skyline always took her breath away. Fog or no fog, the spires of the downtown and the smell of the waterways always drew her back to scenes from her childhood. They had lived only a few blocks away.

"Quarter for your thoughts?"

She answered Eric without turning around. "Nah, they're not for sale."

He took the seat next to her on the park bench. They both faced out toward Fisherman's Wharf.

"Do you still want to help me?" Ava asked.

"Nothing has changed since day before yesterday, so yes."

"This could be a little dangerous."

He chuckled. "I think your definition of dangerous and mine are completely different. I'm pretty sure I can handle your 'dangerous.'"

She turned to face him.

"No, really Eric, I need your help to find out everything you can on a man named Carl Luden—only it's not his real name. We were trying to help his granddaughter. That's the police mess you read about in the papers. You know Johanna. She was only trying to help when she was attacked at the same scene as the murder."

"What! You didn't tell me that the other day."

"Not so loud. We don't know who we're dealing with." She looked around. There were a few people who had come onto the walking trail. One glanced in their direction but kept going. "Except for one local paper the police had kept her name out of the news. But yesterday, the San Francisco papers published Legacy's name. Anyway, I'm worried whoever killed the victim, a man named Phillip Nava, may think Johanna can be a threat. She was there."

"Nava," Eric repeated. "I know him . . . well know of him." Eric slapped the top of his thighs, and shook his head. "Ava, I like Jo and everything, but you have got to look for fewer drama-magnet friends."

"Do you want to help me or not?"

"Of course I do." He grinned and gave her a mock salute. "I got it. Find this Carl Luden."

"No, don't find him. Just find out about him." She reached into her purse and pulled out a folded sheet of paper. "Here's the information Johanna had collected on his business. I can assure you he's not there now."

Eric scanned the page.

"It's not very much."

"I know," Ava agreed grudgingly. "But it's all we've got."

"You said he showed up at your office yesterday?"

"Yes. He was very intimidating, or trying to be," she said. "He said he would get back in touch with us. Oh, and he said he's no longer in the witness protection program. You don't have to look there."

Eric folded his arms across his chest and frowned.

"Don't you find it a little strange someone who has taken such great pains to hide his location and identity over all these years—just walks into your office and shares his feelings for a granddaughter he's never contacted on his own?"

"What are you saying?"

"I'm saying, no, I'm asking, with all this crazy identity switching, how do you know you're talking to the real Carl Luden and not someone who wants to use Legacy as a distraction to help flush the real Luden out of wherever he is?"

Ava smirked. "That's what Johanna said. She doesn't trust this guy one little bit."

CHAPTER TWELVE

JOHANNA WAS THE FIRST TO ARRIVE AT LEGACY in the morning. She turned on the lights as she walked down the short hallway to her office. Since his start, Marty was the one who opened, and closed the office but he had asked for a couple of hours off that morning. He hadn't said why, and she hadn't asked. It was none of her business. Ava had given her thumbs up and he and Trinidad had already formed a bond, and that said a lot.

She had also expressed her concern about Luden's surprise appearance in their office. Johanna agreed it had opened up a trail of alternate possibilities, all unsettling. Was she being used or set up?

Johanna picked through the mail on her desk.

Her phone trilled with the sound of crashing waves.

"Hi, Mom, how are you?"

"I'm fine. Or, I will be when you tell me how you are."

"I'm fine too. What's up?"

Elizabeth Girrard cleared her throat. "I take it you haven't read today's Chronicle?"

"No, I haven't had a chance to scan my e-news yet. Why?"

"You're in it," her mother's voice wavered. "Do you hear me? You're in it, Johanna. They reported it was you out at that house with the murder." She paused. "People will know."

Johanna rubbed the nape of her neck.

Great.

"Well they say all publicity is good publicity," she could hear the lackluster tone in her own voice. "Don't worry Mom, please. The police are on this and . . . and I'm on it too. I'll be careful."

"I don't suppose you would consider staying with me—maybe for just a week?" Her parental plea did not go unnoticed. "It would make me feel so much better, and we could have some fun together . . . like the old days."

Johanna winced. The old days were the days before Johanna's husband and toddler daughter had died in a car crash. The old days were a fantasy, a false sense of joy before the nightmare. The wound was slowly closing but the memory of the pain was still there.

"Let me think on it," Johanna said, pushing her plate away. "I'll get back to you, tomorrow. Love you, Mom. Okay?"

"Okay, but—"

Johanna clicked off.

She wondered if staying at her Mom's would mean she'd have to have breakfast before leaving the house. For sure, she wouldn't be the one to open up the doors in the morning.

Turning on her laptop she clicked to the *San Francisco Chronicle* online edition. Her mother was right. In the first paragraph under the blaring headline: "Wine Country Murder—Family Consultant Discovers Body"—was her name. It was no doubt the reason for the blinking message light next to the nine messages on the land-line. She went through them quickly, none from Leslie.

Trinidad came to her door with a bag of muffins.

"Good morning, Johanna," she said. "If you have coffee, I have muffins. I need to talk to you about my client her—"

"Trinidad, did you read the article in the *Chronicle* this morning?"

The young woman nodded, and leaned against the doorway. "Yes, I saw it. It wasn't bad for us, only unfortunate. I think we will get many calls today."

Johanna agreed. She didn't want to be around for the possible onslaught and packed up her tote. She would hide out in the research room at the county records office.

LESLIE SUMMERS WAS NO EASIER TO FIND than Leslie Todd. She even tried Leslie Luden. After a couple of hours of risking to annoy her favorite records clerk, there wasn't a hint of a trail past what Leslie had already told her. Johanna had encountered circumstances like this before; it just took time. But in this instance she didn't think time was on her side.

When she returned to work, Marty was on the phone, Ava had someone in her office and Trinidad was running copies.

"Hi," Johanna said over the machine whirr. "Everyone seems to be very busy. What are you working on?"

"Ah, Johanna, glad you are back. Don't worry, Ava and Marty knew about the newspaper. We've been getting more calls than usual, but they are not so many now." Trinidad paused in feeding in pages. "I am making copies for Simone Copeland. She comes here today and we go to have lunch with her aunt."

"I'm sorry, you wanted to talk to me about her. Let's do it now."

"No, it is all right. It gave me a chance to think it through for myself. I know how to handle."

"Did her aunt tell you who her father is?"

"Yes and no." she winced. "I think he was the husband of her mother's good friend."

"Oooh, that's awkward."

Johanna shot a second glance at Trinidad dressed in black slacks and a black-striped pale blue silk blouse. There was something different about her.

"What?" Trinidad said, responding to the stare.

"Oh, nothing," Johanna responded, turning to leave and then turning back. "Are you wearing new makeup? You look different today."

"I am same Trinidad," she said, placing the remaining set of pages in the feeder.

"Of course," Johanna said, stepping out of her way.

But something was different.

Then it struck her, Trinidad was wearing blue.

Two hours later, she rubbed her eyes, she could hear Ava in the lobby saying goodbye to her clients. She entered Johanna's office and flopped in the chair in front of her desk.

"Well the Pattison's are both happy. He apologized for thinking family trees were a waste of time—particularly after he found out he had a famous cousin who was trying to get in touch with him." Ava smiled, sipping from her cup of coffee. "And she's delighted she can pass on heritage information to their children.

"Keep those happy clients coming," she said. Then, she pushed away her keyboard. "You haven't asked me about searching for Leslie Todd, or this whole nightmarish situation splashed in the *Chronicle.*"

"Because I know if you had results or something to say, you'd let me know."

"True, and I don't."

"So, I take it the trip to the Vallejo courthouse was uneventful?"

"Did you know they are thirty-three Leslie Summers born between 2005 and 1995? And, twenty-four Leslie Todds?" Johanna put elbows on the desk and held her chin in her hands."

"So, uneventful is a yes?"

Johanna exhaled and nodded.

"It's going to take some time. I've asked Marty to work with Trinidad and start checking deeper background so I can work with a shorter list." She furrowed her brow. "But there's something else. Nick wants to talk to me, again, this time over lunch about Philip Nava. I told him everything I remember but he thinks that I may have overlooked a detail."

"Well, at least you'll get a lunch out of it."

THEY HAD ORDERED SANDWICHES, but both were untouched.

"Johanna, I know you've given your statement, but we're hoping that with the time passing you might remember something else."

Detective Nick Quinn sat across from her, his face drawn and his hands clenched. "Other than your DNA and prints, we can't find a record on anyone else. We're running down Nava's doings but while his leads are long, his recent activities are slim. And all we run into with the name Carl Luden are dead ends. But that makes sense if he was in the Marshall's program."

Johanna's eyes widened. But she said nothing.

"You just thought of something," he pressed. "What was it?"

"In my statement I said I sensed it was a male that pushed me," she mused. "I still think so but I've been thinking since Leslie Todd hasn't contacted me, she might have been in on it."

"We thought that too, but since she didn't know where you two were driving, how would she have known how to hook up with Nava's killer?"

"Unless *she* was in on it with Nava's killer. How do we know she didn't fake not knowing the location? I mean she insisted on driving," Johanna said. She moistened her lips. "Uh . . . Nick, I had a brief, very brief meeting with Carl Luden earlier this week. He came to our office."

"You what!"

"It came to nothing." She scrambled for her explanation at the detectives obvious agitation. "He says he didn't kill Nava, but he had to get away because he knew we would contact the police and there would be media. I told him the police still wanted to speak with him. But he said it was too risky. He wants me to make contact with granddaughter. He wants to explain what's been happening and why."

Nick rubbed his eye brows and stared at her.

"Great, we'd like to know that too. You know you're obstructing a police investigation," he said. "I just happened to offer to take you to lunch. When were you going to tell me about your meeting? We have a northern California-wide search for Luden and you just let him walk through your hands."

He continued, "How did Legacy get involved with Leslie Todd

and Carl Luden? What do you know?" His voice was low and controlled—not a good sign.

She went over the Luden conversation, but stopped mid-sentence. "Johanna, what is it?"

"Carl Luden is not his real name, you know that. It's the name he gave himself when he left protection," Johanna said. "You have to think if he changes names that easily, he could likely do the same again."

TRINIDAD

TRINIDAD SNUCK A SIDE GLANCE AT SIMONE sitting in the passenger seat and chewing absently on the baby finger of her left hand. Her eyes returned to the highway. She'd just gotten her driver's license and her cousin, Lincoln, had gifted her his old Honda. She felt in charge.

"It is going to be all right, Simone."

"What? Oh, I know it will be. What could go wrong?" She waved her hand in the air.

"That is exactly the way to see it," Trinidad said. "Knowing is always better than not knowing—most of the time. Mrs. Copeland may seem to be a little . . . a little . . . mmm . . . gruff. I think is the word. But she is candy inside." Even as the words left her lips, Trinidad wondered if the comparison to candy was overdoing it.

When they arrived, it was clear Jane must have been assigned to freshen up the pathway entrance to the door. It had been swept and dead blooms pinched from the frail flowers. The dog poop had been removed and the population of flies had migrated with it.

Simone, still unsure, stood to her left and behind Trinidad as she rang the bell. Jane opened the door as if she had been waiting for their arrival.

"Come in, Ms. Copeland is in the living room." Jane grinned and pointed to the room off the entry. "She's very excited."

She stretched out her hand to Simone who shook it gingerly.

"We are excited too, Jane." Trinidad said gesturing. "Simone, this is the young woman I told you is helping your aunt. I—"

A voice called out.

"Stop blabbering, I'm waiting. What's going on out there?"

Jane shrugged apologetically at the two guests and ushered them into the room.

"Hello, Ms. Copeland, I bring your niece to see you." Trinidad smiled and stepped aside motioning Simone ahead.

The young woman held a shy smile and edged forward, just as Audrey Copeland rolled her chair back and tilted her head with a frown. Her lips formed a pencil thin line. Her eyes squinted peering at Simone as if viewing a statue.

"Who are you?" Copeland sneered.

"Mrs. Copeland, this is . . ." Trinidad stuttered. She sensed more than saw Simone's readiness to take flight. "This is Simone, your niece, Tanya's daughter. Remember, you wanted us to visit you."

"She's not anything to me." Copeland was all but yelling, pointing her finger. "But I know who you are. She lied, she lied. I'd know those green eyes anywhere. Get out. Get out of my house both of you."

Copeland swirled her chair around and pushed into the hallway this time making contact with Jane's foot. Jane jumped back with a wince of pain on her face.

Trinidad didn't try to hide her puzzlement. But she was even more taken back at the sound of the next words.

"Wait, I can explain," Simone called after the retreating figure.

THERE WAS SILENCE IN THE CAR AS THEY STARTED the drive back to the East Bay, until Trinidad couldn't take it anymore.

"What happened back there, Simone?" She blurted. "What do you mean 'you can explain'? I would like to know that explanation. Please, tell me now."

"I'm sorry Trinidad, I know I should have told you, but . . . but I was afraid you wouldn't take me to see her," Simone's voice quivered. "I've been trying to find Aunt Audrey ever since my Mom died." She paused. "It's hard to explain."

Trinidad shook her head.

"No, Simone it is not hard to explain. It is simple. Start talking now, please."

Simone nodded.

"Everything I told you is true. I am dying from a disease which is passed down from both parents. And, I know the man who is listed on my birth certificate is not my father." She paused. "When the doctor told me, to hear those words, I was . . . I was traumatized."

Again, she paused as if remembering the moment.

"But they were both gone . . . dead. I had no one to ask," Simone's voice broke. "My mother and I were close . . . but I guess not close enough."

"Simone," Trinidad cleared her throat. "Did you think your aunt would be able to tell you who your father is? But, why did she act so strongly—so angry?"

"It's my eyes."

"Your eyes?"

They exchanged a quick glance. Simone's emerald green eyes were filling with tears. Trinidad gripped the steering wheel.

"What about your eyes, Simone? What are you trying to tell me?" "I have my father's eyes," she said staring at her hands in her lap. "I was throwing out some old papers of my Mom and I found a letter—a note really, my mother wrote to a friend when I was born. It said I had my father's eyes," her voice lowered. "The man who raised me, who I thought was my father had brown eyes."

"Oh, but these things happen." Trinidad shrugged. "So you knew the man on the certificate was not your father. And then the doctors told you so. I do not understand the reaction of your aunt."

"I didn't know for sure . . .," her voice drifted. Then she straightened. "Aunt Audrey and my mother did not get along. When my mother died, she didn't even attend the funeral. Now, after . . . after her seeing . . . after seeing my eyes . . . this confirms my father was her husband."

CHAPTER THIRTEEN

JOHANNA SENSED SHE WAS BEING WATCHED. Even though there was no one visible on the street, her survivor instinct had kicked in. There was still someone out there.

Her weekend had gone by quickly filled with household chores and research on the U.S. Marshall Court procedures. The break gave her a clear head. But now on guard, she purposely dropped a file on the sidewalk from the folder she was carrying, and then quickly turned to look up.

There was no one to see. Maybe it was too much television.

Gathering the papers to her chest, she hurried to the building's entry. The lobby wasn't busy. There were only a few people waiting for the elevator, and two women talking avidly while huddled in visitor chairs.

"Mrs. Hudson."

Johanna swirled around to the source of the low heavy voice, and nodded to the security guard at reception.

"Yes, what is it?"

"Perhaps we can meet in a less public place?" The man had a solid stomach paunch which stretched his blue shirt over his barely belted waist. His thick glasses magnified his beady brown eyes. He lifted the frames.

"Mr. Luden?" She found herself whispering. "I didn't recognize you. Do you work here? Where's Thomas?" Johanna stretched to look on the floor behind the desk.

It was as if he read her mind.

"Mrs. Hudson, I didn't hurt your friend. He's checking on his car. He'll be back in about . . ." He looked at his watch. "Five minutes—we don't have much time. There is a water fountain at the plaza near Pleasanton's fair grounds not far from here. It's open to the public, we'll be able to talk in private. You know it?"

She nodded. Luden motioned with his head.

"He's on his way back. We can catch up this evening. Don't contact the police, at least not yet. Make it 4:30." Turning from her, he came from around the desk and waved to a grateful Thomas. "It's all yours man."

Johanna watched him trudge out the rear doors to the parking lot.

"Anything I can help you with?" Thomas settled in his seat.

"No." She shook her head. "I got my answer."

"CARL LUDEN WAS IN THE BUILDING?" Marty scowled.

"Johanna, what did he want?" This was Ava's second time asking the question. "Thank God you were in a public place. You should never meet with him alone. The man could be a killer."

"He just wanted to know if I had made progress getting in touch with his granddaughter." Johanna didn't look Ava in the eye. The woman was a walking lie detector device. "I told him we didn't have anything confirmed."

She could feel the tension in the small break room, which was one of the reasons she withheld the truth. Leslie was counting on her. She didn't want to give her trusting client another reason to feel abandoned. For some reason, she believed Carl Luden, or whatever his name was. And, she couldn't think of any reason she could give to make Ava and Marty understand.

"So he went to all the trouble of wearing a disguise, risking discovery just to ask a question which could have been accomplished with a phone call?" Ava's skepticism was evident. "Have you even heard from Leslie?"

"I don't know his motives and no, I haven't heard from Leslie," Johanna said. "We all need to stay on guard." She looked down at her fitness watch. "Oops, I've got to write out some ideas for Trinidad. And, I told my mother I would help her pick out some drapes, so I'll be leaving a little early."

Marty nodded and headed back to his desk.

Ava filled her cup with coffee and casually took a sip while blocking Johanna's exit.

"You don't fool me; you're lying. Your mother has more design sense than all of us put together."

JOHANNA ARRIVED AT THE PLAZA A LITTLE EARLY. She could see the water feature from her parking space. There were no other cars there. At 4:30 she got out and headed for the concrete seating around the fountain.

She recognized the trim figure if not the face, as Luden approached wearing a grey jogging suit and walking a cocker-doodle pulling at the leash. He sat about three feet from her, as if in casual conversation.

"Thank you for trusting me," he said.

"I don't."

He nodded in understanding.

"That's fair." his voice was calm and matter of fact as he stared out over the park. "Twenty years ago, I was marked a dead man. In exchange for evidence, the Feds had promised immunity and a new identity for me and my family. It was my ticket out. But it was a jump from one hell to another. They couldn't protect me enough. I got out of the program when my whereabouts was leaked, and I ran with my family. I decided neither my old cronies nor the government would have any more control over my life. I would mark my own course."

"And the evidence, was it money?"

He jerked his head toward her his eyes narrowed, and his jaw tightened.

"What do you know about the money?"

"I don't until you just admitted it." Johanna gave a crooked smile. "But there had to be for you to get witness protection, relocate a family and start a new life. That's not cheap—and I don't expect your 'old cronies' continue to look for you because they're planning a reunion."

"Well, not the kind I'd look forward to." He chuckled, but not with his eyes. "My granddaughter is all that's left of my family. We weren't all that close when she was growing up. I tried. My daughter, her mother and I . . . we could never get on the right footing. That's another reason why I had to get out of the protection program."

Johanna frowned with impatience.

"Let's get back to Leslie," she said. "What's going on? And why all of a sudden do you want to get in touch with a long-lost granddaughter. She was the one who made the initial effort."

"You ask a lot of questions."

Johanna shrugged.

"I'll add one more. Who was Phillip Nava?"

This time Luden's face flushed an angry red. Johanna stiffened when a vein at his temple became engorged. Then suddenly, like a flipped light switch, he exhaled and a mask of calm slid over his expression.

"Nava was trash. He deserved to die."

"But you didn't kill him?"

"Nope," Luden replied. "Somebody got there before I did."

She tried her best not to look shocked at his words. Instead she cleared her throat.

"What did he do?"

Eyes narrowed, Luden looked away. "He was a greedy criminal." He paused. "My . . . a . . . friend . . . A friend of mine couldn't see him for what he was."

She tapped her bottom lip with her finger then tilted her head as she stared at the man next to her, who was now engrossed in rubbing his knuckles. She shook her head.

"No, not a friend of yours—it was Leslie wasn't it?" Johanna said with mounting assurance supported by Luden's slowly stiffening jaw. "Nava was her fiancé. He was going to marry your granddaughter. If he was as bad as you say, you couldn't afford to have him in the family. You didn't want anyone to make the connection between her and you. Did Leslie know he was working for you?"

He squinted into the distance. "He threatened to tell her."

"Mr. Luden, I'm a little confused. Let me see if I have this right. Leslie told Nava that she was looking for her history—her long lost grandfather. He wanted to flush you out, it was about the money. He knew Leslie had an inheritance. He wanted a share or maybe as you say he was greedy enough to want it all. But he didn't know he had to get in line."

Finally he muttered, "They want me to know they have her under their sights. They want the money they think I got away with. They are willing to kill for it. They killed Nava."

Johanna's eyes widened. Her hand was beginning to shake, a PTSD trait that hadn't occurred since her own capture and rescue previous months ago from a psychopath. Why now, she asked herself—and almost immediately had the answer— because, she knew without a doubt, if she continued down this path she might not be so lucky this time.

She noticed Luden was waiting for her to say something. She cleared her throat.

"Why are you telling me these things? You don't know me. How do you know you can trust me? You spent twenty years hiding behind a false background. Why risk throwing it all away revealing this to me?"

He rubbed the top of his thighs.

"Eric said you were the real deal."

"Eric!"

AVA

AVA LOOKED ACROSS THE MUSEUM GALLERY and then down at her Fitbit for the umpteenth time—three o'clock. Eric was many things but he was not someone who made an appointment and didn't show, or call. He was over an hour late. Pacing, then sitting, then pacing again, she settled on one end of a viewing bench and an earnest-looking young woman staring at the Modigliani, sat on the other end.

Eric had called her late last night to ask her to meet him at the San Francisco Museum of Modern Art.

"Why the museum?" she asked.

He had chuckled. "Because that's where spies meet." He paused. Then, in a lowered tone, "Seriously, Ava, I think I stumbled onto something about Luden. I want to run it past you. But to get it, unfortunately, I had to show a few cards. Usually I'd ask you out to dinner, but I think it best if I visit those friends in Hawaii after we talk. I'll take the package to Aunt Lillian. Could you give me a ride to the airport?"

Begrudgingly, she had agreed to both requests if only to satisfy her curiosity. Still, his wariness clearly shown in his voice. She sighed at never being able to say no to him.

Her phone buzzed.

Trinidad.

"Ava, you should come back to the office. The police are here. They are going through your desk. They have warrant."

Ava stood abruptly.

"The police are in my office!" she called out.

Her museum bench mate looked up in alarm and then gathering her backpack, moved away.

"Yes, Ava, they are here, but Johanna is not. We didn't see a reason why they couldn't search. Marty is here but they put he and me in the coffee room to stay out of the way. There is a police looking at me right now. But, there is more, Ava, much more."

Ava was already half-running toward the exit sign.

"Wait," Trinidad ordered. "Marty wants to speak at you . . . I mean speak to you."

She could hear the phone hand-off.

His voice sounded rushed. "Ava, you need to get back here."

"Marty, what is going on?"

"The police say that Eric Lowell is missing."

SHE DIDN'T KNOW HOW SHE ARRIVED at Legacy's parking lot. There had to have been traffic signals and pedestrians, but she couldn't recall. It must have been muscle memory. She had driven blindly through the flush of tears she didn't try to stop, even if she could. As if on a recording loop, all she could remember were Marty's words: ". . . he's missing."

Eric was missing. What does that even mean? It's only been a day since they spoke. The only man she ever loved—probably still loved, could be missing or maybe even dead?

Entering the building, she dashed up the steps, the elevator was too slow.

Why were the police in her office?

The office entry door was open with a uniformed officer standing guard.

In the lobby, Ava rushed up to a man and a woman, not in uniform, with heads together over an open folder. She could see past them to an officer in her office checking behind one of her hanging diplomas.

Good grief.

"Mrs. Lowell?" The woman asked.

Ava nodded.

"My name is Detective Amy Warner. We want to thank you for your cooperation in allowing us to search your office. Your staff said it would be no problem. We would like to retrieve your laptop and any other electronic accessories—including your phone. It's just to eliminate you from our inquiries." She handed Ava a sheet of paper, and then held out her hand. "You should be able to pick everything up tomorrow—or the day after."

"What? Why?" Ava stuttered, digging in her purse for her phone.

Warner continued to speak. "This is Detective Chris Holt," she said, "We are assigned to this case. We have reason to believe that you, and named others, are persons of interest in the disappearance of your husband Eric Lowell."

"Ex-husband—but how . . . why are you *here*?" Ava dropped her phone in a proffered plastic bag.

Holt stepped forward. "Your husband—sorry, ex-husband—went missing yesterday afternoon," he spoke in a clipped tone. "His last call was to you. He was supposed to meet with the police early afternoon, but he never showed up. He broke off suddenly on a call to them. He said after he had some pertinent conversations with you, he had made some critical discoveries that would implicate a number of shady characters in a deal to defraud the government. Some witnesses saw him shoved into an unmarked van."

He looked over her head and nodded. Ava stood aside as he moved past her to enter her office.

"But I don't understand, why—"

"Mrs. Lowell, are you aware your ex-husband was a potential black mailer and he had implicated you in—"

"Don't answer that, Ava."

Johanna charged into the room, frowning at the police guard. "I understand from my . . . my partner . . .," Johanna nodded down the hall at Trinidad's insistent finger pointing from the coffee room doorway. "That . . . that Ava has been falsely . . . er . . . labeled . . . er a person of interest in . . . ah, some crime. And if you have what you came for, then you should just . . . just go."

"Are you an attorney?" Warner asks.

"Uh, no," Johanna said. "But, I know her rights to contact an attorney, and Ava is my friend."

Ava stood to the side as if turned to stone.

Warner shook her head and held out a card. "Tell your friend," she said, "we would like to interview her in our office tomorrow morning at 9 a.m. Do you understand, Mrs. Lowell, with or without your attorney?" She waited for Ava's nod and motioned to the officer blocking the coffee room doorway to come forward.

Holt returned to the lobby with another officer carrying a number of files including Ava's desktop computer and laptop. They all left.

Trinidad, followed by Marty, stood next to Ava, her arm across her shoulder. Johanna closed the door and pointed to the chairs and they all sat. Johanna slipped her jacket off.

"What the hell is going on?"

Ava turned to her. "Eric is missing. I think they presume he is dead."

"What!" Johanna exclaimed. She leaned over to squeeze Ava's hand. "Oh, I'm so sorry, Ava. What happened?"

"That's all I know, they wouldn't tell me anymore." Ava burst into tears. "If Marty hadn't called to tell me about Eric . . . and the search, I would still be waiting to meet him at the museum. Oh, my . . . I just can't believe this." She dabbed her eyes with a tissue.

Johanna squinted. "Could we just back up a bit? You were meeting Eric at a museum?"

Ava nodded and slowly explained the recent assignment for her ex.

"He was only supposed to find out who Carl Luden was, he wasn't to contact him. I made it really clear. But . . . but he always has to show off . . . he . . . he always *used* to show off, he . . ." her voice trickled to silence.

Trinidad cleared her throat. "I am used to police. In my birth country they are everywhere. Here, the police come to the door. We know Ava has nothing to hide. There is nothing we can do. As soon as we can, we call Ava. Then Marty call Johanna."

"Yeah, but they didn't have me fooled. It was better to give them access," Marty leaned over, elbows on thighs. "Ava, they might also show up at your home?"

She didn't miss Johanna giving him a sinking look.

"No . . . they didn't say anything . . . I . . ." Ava's woeful look bespoke her misery.

Johanna patted her friend on the back. "Stay with me tonight. We'll go get some of your things. I need to talk to you about a conversation I just had with Carl Luden." She pulled her purse onto her shoulder. "I'll contact Nick and ask him to tell us what he can. Then we'll talk to Dean Cameron. He helped us before when Trinidad had trouble last year. You're not going to a police interview without an attorney.

"Will you come with me tomorrow?" Ava turned to look into Johanna's eyes.

"You don't even have to ask." Johanna reassured. "Now let's get you home."

CHAPTER FOURTEEN

THE POLICE HAD ALREADY COME AND GONE when she and Ava arrived at the condo and packed her overnight bag. They left a card in the door with their number to respond. Hardly speaking, the two headed straight back to Johanna's townhome. Ava seemed completely deflated. She only wanted to crawl into bed. Downstairs, Johanna went into the kitchen to make her calls.

"The case was assigned to another team. Detectives Ward and Howell are okay," Nick said in reply to her questions. "They're by the book, so no concern in that corner."

She must have caught Nick just as he arrived at home. She could hear him turn the key in the lock.

"Nick, I was hoping . . . I was wondering if you could find out what they have on Ava. She has to meet with them in the morning and—"

"No, I can't. I play it by the book, too."

"Okay, then tell me this. What should I infer, from what has transpired so far with the confiscation of her personal items and everything . . . by the book I mean?"

"Johanna, don't get snarky," he said. "First, her items were not confiscated, she gave permission. Second, it's not my case and third, I can't show special treatment." He exhaled. "Look, from what you're telling me I would surmise Eric Lowell had some evidence pointing to Ava as being an associate in some deal gone bad and—"

"That's nuts. Ava would never—"

"Let me finish," he said calmly. "But, it doesn't sound like what they have is a slam dunk. That's why they needed to see what they could find from Ava. When Ava comes in tomorrow, tell her to just tell the truth and that she and Eric are no longer together."

There was silence.

"Johanna, are you still there?"

"Yes, but . . . uh . . . Ava still talked with Eric every so often."

"When was the last 'often', and what was it about?"

"I'm not absolutely sure, but I think she told me she met with him about a week ago and . . . and asked him for a favor."

"A favor?"

"To help her get information on this . . . person. You see, there's this client we have . . . a granddaughter looking for the identity of her grandfather, at least we thought that was it. Then it turns out the grandfather is looking for his granddaughter—our client may have misled us and . . ." she stopped to take a breath. "Anyway, I know it sounds confusing, even more so when a guy was murdered in the grandfather's house."

"What? Slow down, too many details," Nick responded. "Wait, this situation sounds familiar. Does this have anything to do with the Nava killing? Did you know Eric Lowell too?"

Johanna got up from her chair to take a peek up the stairs to make sure Ava's door was still closed.

"Hold on, Nick, now you have too many questions," Johanna replied returning to her chair. "I don't know . . . yes . . . and I don't know. Those are my answers."

This time Nick was silent for moments before he spoke.

"You got her an attorney, right?"

It was her next call.

JOHANNA CALLED DEAN CAMERON, AN ATTORNEY who had helped to rescue Trinidad from her legal issues the previous year. The last twenty-four, make that eighteen hours, had been a roller coaster ride.

"Of course, I'll help Ava. I know Detective Ward, he's diligent and smart. I've worked with him before," Dean said. "But tell Ava not to talk to anyone until I've spoken with her. I'll see you both at Legacy in the morning."

Later, Johanna had no problem getting Ava to agree to remain silent, but it was a struggle getting her to take a breath and push away the dread that had settled on her face.

"Johanna, I just want to pull the blanket over my head and crawl into a ball. This is my entire fault. I wasn't able to get a hold of him. I told him to go after Luden."

"No, you told him to find out what he could without contacting Luden's comrades. You told him it could be dangerous."

Ava shook her head in denial. "You and I both know Eric well enough to know any caution I gave him was like waving a red flag in front of a bull."

DEAN CAMERON PRESSED ON SPEAKING ALONE with Ava, despite her wanting Johanna to join them in the small office at the police station.

"As her attorney, I'm going to have to insist in this instance, I only speak with Ava." Dean said, giving Johanna an acknowledging nod. "After this, you can accompany her whenever she wants you."

"Go ahead, Ava." Johanna nudged. "You don't have much time. It's almost eight-thirty. I'll join you and Dean in the police interview room."

Ava frowned, but gestured she accepted the inevitable. The door closed behind them.

JOHANNA RETURNED TO THE LOBBY and checked her email. What had Eric found out? She wavered in wanting to trust Luden and yet wary he may not be who he says he is. Clearly Eric had stumbled on something. And, there was Eric, how did he know Luden? Luden realized he had slipped the name and refused to say more. It was that revelation more than anything else, taking place in the last day that shook Johanna the most.

Eric and Carl Luden knew each other.

AFTER ALMOST AN HOUR OF QUESTIONING in the cold sterile police interview room, Johanna was waved in. She entered and sat next to Ava. Detectives Ward and Howell traded glances at Ava who was sitting stiffly in a chair. Johanna moved closer.

"Thank you for your time, Mrs. Lowell," Ward said. "You can go."

The detectives stood and collected their papers.

"What about her things, her computers and phone?" Dean asked.

Howell responded from the doorway, "We're not quite through with them. If we don't have any more questions, you should be able to pick everything up about this time tomorrow."

Then, they were gone.

Ava dropped her head into her hands. Johanna put her arms around her.

"What happens now?" Johanna asked Dean.

"Let's talk outside." He said, holding the door for Ava and Johanna.

He led them at a brisk pace to a visitor table and park bench and put his hand on Ava's shoulder as they sat down.

"Ava, you remember what we talked about this morning, right?"

Ava nodded robotically.

"No talking to anyone, not even Johanna," he insisted.

"I understand." Ava replied looking woefully at her friend.

He held up his hand in anticipation of a protest. "I don't want them to extend their investigation to you, Johanna. As long as you can truthfully say you have no knowledge of Eric Lowell's activities, the better off Ava will be."

"All right," Johanna responded. "But, since *I don't* have any knowledge of Eric's activities, can't you tell me generally what's going on? What's Ava being accused of?"

"Yes, of course," he said, giving a glance to Ava who seemed unable to stop staring at Johanna. "The police think Eric Lowell has gone underground because he was somehow connected to Philip Nava. They found evidence pointing to Lowell having contacted someone he thought might know Luden. It is this person that turned out to be either Nava's murderer or a Luden ally, or both. Adding to the Keystone Cops background, over eager, Lowell contacted your friend, Detective Nick Quinn, offering to get close to Luden and turn informant. He referenced Ava as his source, thinking dropping her name would legitimatize his offer."

"Oh, you have got to be kidding." Johanna said.

Ava sat shaking her head.

Dean continued, "The feds have taken jurisdiction. The Sheriff's Office is performing support. Frankly, I don't think either of them think that Eric Lowell is a major player. But there is enough smoke and fire to keep him on their list as a person of interest. They are hard after Luden, but all they have is Lowell, and now they don't have him."

Johanna partially covered her mouth with her hand.

"Dean, I know Eric. He was a little dodgy at times but never anything really criminal." Johanna frowned. "And other than Eric using Ava's name, how does Ava fit in the picture?"

"I can't go into that, but until they find out what happened to Eric Lowell they assume he could be working with Luden's gang. Evidently, Lowell had notes from his conversation with Ava when she asked him to get information on Carl Luden."

"Wrote it down!" Johanna exclaimed. "No, way, Eric was not that meticulous. Besides I think he still loves Ava, he would never incriminate her."

"Johanna is right. It didn't happen like that," Ava blurted. "I keep telling them I only asked him to find out what he could."

Tears were once more brimming under Ava's lids. Johanna passed her a packet of tissue.

Dean waved a hand in deference.

"I've asked to see these 'notes'. Evidently, the police have their doubts, too." Dean let out a slow breath. "It may take a little while, but once they verify she doesn't have any information, they'll move on. But, until they do, I want her to lie low, stay close and keep quiet."

Dean said his goodbyes and left for his car. Johanna and Ava exchanged worried looks, and then almost simultaneously they uttered:

"What do we tell Trinidad and Marty?"

CHAPTER FIFTEEN

THEIR DRIVE BACK TO THE OFFICE was spent practicing various plausible explanations to Marty and Trinidad for Ava's predicament. They decided on the truth.

"We'll tell them what Dean told me," Johanna said pulling out of the parking space. The lot was almost empty at the end of the day. "It keeps them out of trouble."

"What about Luden?" Ava's voice had regained its composure once out of site of the city jail. "Why is he anxious to finally meet his granddaughter all of a sudden?"

Johanna wrinkled her forehead.

"We'll keep trying to reach Leslie Todd. I want to make sure she's okay," Johanna said her eyes on the roadway. "She wanted us to find her grandfather. If she's changed her mind I want to know for sure." Johanna turned to look at her passenger. "There is one thing though, Ava."

Ava looked expectantly at her. "What?"

"Leslie was involved with Nava."

Ava closed her eyes and pressed the back of her head into the headrest.

"Of course she was."

IN THE OFFICE COFFEE ROOM, JOHANNA caught the looks between Trinidad and Marty.

"I've got to process this," he said sipping from his coffee mug. He got up to get a refill.

Trinidad nodded. "I not sure what process is, but I think we need to think about this and decide how we will do business."

"What do you mean, Trini?" Ava asked.

"Well, are you still going to Australia?"

"Oh, my God, I'd totally put it out of my head." Ava put her hand to her mouth. "And I made my air reservations to leave in two weeks."

Johanna put her hand over Ava's. "It's not likely the police will allow you to go."

"I agree with Johanna," Marty said. "I know how much it means to you, but from what you told us, Ava, the police will want you to stay close."

"Wait," Johanna said. "There's a chance that the police will determine that your role was only as a bystander. I'll talk to Nick maybe he—"

"No. First, I'm returning to my condo." Ava shook her head. "Second, you're all correct. The police are not going to let me go with a cloud of suspicion hanging over my head. Third, while this is a dig assignment of my lifetime, I wouldn't be able to concentrate." Her eyes renewed with tears. "I'll have to wait it out."

TRINIDAD

TRINIDAD SAT IN THE LOBBY AND took out her phone to glance at the time. Simone should arrive soon. They had agreed to meet at the county clerk's office and request copies of her birth records together. Fortunately, the county had received a grant to fund genealogical assistance needed by adoptees. Of course there was paperwork to qualify. Like in her own birth country there was someone whose job it was to create paperwork.

"Hi, Trinidad," Simone said approaching her from the east and for a moment the sun's glare blocked her features.

Trinidad rose and looked into the crystal green eyes that declared her birthright.

"Hello Simone, are you ready to start?" she asked reaching out to touch her arm. "We will be meeting with an advocate who will walk you through the system and program. But, you do not have to go forward. You can stop at any time."

"No." Simone gave her a tentative smile. "I'm ready. I want to meet my father."

"Yes, it is good."

Trinidad only hoped he wanted to meet her.

TRINIDAD NOTICED THE TREMBLE in Simone's voice who answered as many questions as she could directed by a middle-aged woman in jeans and matching jacket. The advocate committed to returning with an initial review of documents and hopefully the name of Simone's father.

Trinidad didn't tell Simone that she too was close to finding out her father's name. Audrey Copeland and taken back her maiden name, but her marital records were still out there. It would just take a little time to track him down.

"If things fall into place easily," the older woman paused then continued. "I may hear back from him and learn if he may be interested in seeing you." Noticing Simone's grin she added, "However, you should not count on that happening. There is a 50-50 chance, for reasons of his own, after all this time, he does not wish to be reminded of his past and will want to remain silent."

Simone's face went crestfallen.

"You will let us know what you find, yes?" Trinidad said.

"Of course, it is one of the criteria allowing me to talk to you."

Their meeting concluded with the advocate reassuring Simone she would be in touch, one way or the other.

Simone was silent on the drive to the lot where she had parked her car. Trinidad snuck glances at the young woman who stared straight ahead.

"Simone, you do not look well. You must not worry," she said. "Soon we know who your father is. Next, we will find him."

"I'm not so sure of that."

"Why do you say this?"

"Suppose the reason he never contacted me wasn't because he didn't want to know me, but, because he already died from the disease he passed on."

Trinidad frowned and considered which outcome would be worse.

WHEN SHE RETURNED TO THE OFFICE, Marty was busy handling a client. She could tell it was a new referral because he was using his radio announcer voice.

"And now, perhaps you'd like to hear our list of extended services..."

Trinidad gave him a smile and a quick wave as she went to her office. Neither Johanna nor Ava were in their rooms which was good she needed time to think about Simone. She plopped in her chair and commenced to slowly swivel over and over.

"What's the matter?" Marty asked from the doorway.

Caught. She gave him a sheepish grin.

"I am thinking, Marty."

"About being a whirling dervish?"

"I do not know what that means, but from your voice I am thinking you are making a joke about me."

"Well maybe a little one," he grinned, taking the seat in front of her desk. The smile left his face and he ran his hand over his hair. "Trini, there's something I'm going to tell you, but I want you to keep it quiet, ah, secret and I'm going to need your help."

"Marty, I can keep a secret." She leaned forward. "I know what *that* means. What is the secret?"

"Johanna is out with Ava trying to re-trace Eric Lowell's steps.

Ava's office is still a mess and I was trying to help put things back. " He rubbed his hand over his face. "I finally got it done. It's pretty quiet today. I had to clear all of the files—"

"Marty, please," Trinidad blurted. "What is the secret?"

He straightened in his chair.

"I want to be more than a receptionist, I want to be like you." He pointed his finger on the desk. "I'm going to solve client's cases."

"What!"

"I said—"

"I know what you said, Marty I am sitting here in front of you. I can tell joke also." Trinidad shook her head. "You are too young and you have only been here a small time. What are you thinking? I make an assistant because I help Legacy with clients. I show them that I was more than a receptionist. And you . . ."

"And, I'm really good at creating file folders." He gave her a knowing smile. "Thanks, Trini. But, I can do more, and I plan on showing Johanna and Ava that they need a field detective—me."

"A field detective!" She said, slamming her back into her chair. "This is not a detective business, Marty. We help people find their families and backgrounds. We do not solve crimes. I know sometimes it looks like it, but . . . well. It is good you are thinking ahead, but you need to do this job first."

He stood, letting the chair roll back to hit the wall.

"I hear you loud and clear, Trini," he moved to the doorway. "You sound like my parents. I shouldn't overreach—don't dream."

"I sound like your parents!" Trinidad repeated. "We are almost the same age. I could be your sister—maybe. But, no, not your mother." She grimaced and then murmured, "Maybe your older sister."

She looked up, squinting in thought, but Marty had left.

CHAPTER SIXTEEN

"**W**HAT EXACTLY DO YOU WANT TO know?" The elderly woman replied not turning her head from the television screen.

Johanna took another deep breath, and then caught it. The combined smell of Pine Sol and a floral air freshener was not a chemical success. She hoped this house call wasn't a waste of time. Leslie Todd had provided her address as the house Nava owned, according to property tax records. Johanna gambled Leslie may have established some relationship with Nava's neighbors, even if a negative one. However, Johanna, after twenty-minutes with next door neighbor Mrs. Eloise Carson, age eighty-eight, she hadn't made it past an introduction.

"I'm a genealogist and I'm trying to track my client's ancestors. I just want to know if you remember your neighbor Phillip Nava and his fiancé, Leslie. He lived next door and she may have stayed there as well."

"A gene . . . a genie. . ., it's a tough job to pronounce. Do you have something to do with garage doors?"

"No, not at all. I—"

"Well, if you're here about Mr. Nava, there's not much I can tell you. They haven't lived here for over . . . let me think . . . The new fire station was built two years ago, and they were here then, so I guess it's been a year since they left. Doesn't matter, they usually kept their garage door closed."

Johanna struggled to rise from the low and deeply over-stuffed upholstered arm chair.

"Mrs. Carson, I want to thank you for seeing me," she said making it awkwardly to her feet. "I'll leave you to enjoy the rest of—"

The old woman pursed her lips and finally looked up to meet Johanna's eyes.

"Now, my husband he loves cars and at eighty-four—he doesn't like people to know I'm older than he is, he still reads car magazines. Anyway, he's an honorary member of our neighborhood watch group. He memorizes every car. He might be able to tell you about Mr. Nava's garage door. I didn't know the house was up for sale. No one else has moved in yet."

Johanna sighed. It would be easy to go down the rabbit hole, but she would close the last loop since she was there.

"Where can I find your husband?"

Larry Carson was perched on the back deck that overlooked a velvety-green golf course. Binoculars in hand, he turned to glance at Johanna when he heard his wife's shuffled approach.

"Larry, this lady wants to see you about garage door openers."

His lips turned down.

"We don't want any."

Johanna came forward. "Mr. Carson, I don't sell garage door openers. I—"

"No, not for us," his wife interjected. "She's talking about that Nava man next door."

"He definitely doesn't want any." He answered, and peered at Johanna. "I'm assuming my wife has got things backwards again. Why *are* you here?"

"Mr. Carson, I'm a genealogist. I've been hired to do an ancestry search for my client." Johanna rushed her explanation to correct the missed communication. "Leslie Todd thought you might be able to help me."

Johanna played a little with the truth. She was disinclined to identify her client as her search target.

"Leslie?" Larry Carson said, putting the field glasses to his eyes. "She was a nice lady. Didn't see her a lot, but she usually made an effort to speak."

"There, you have your answer." Mrs. Carson raised her hand. "I'm going back to my game show." She turned and hobbled back down the hallway.

Johanna took steps to exit out the rear yard, the fresh air was welcome. "Well, thank you for your time, Mr. Carson."

He grunted.

"She was nice, but he was an asshole."

Johanna stopped. He had not taken the binoculars down.

"Mr. Carson, do you know how I can get in touch with Leslie? Her family is looking for her."

"All of a sudden people are trying to find Leslie." He put the glasses in his lap and scrutinized her. "The police were here a couple of days ago—now you. She doesn't know anything about the man's murder, so leave her alone."

Johanna raised an eyebrow and reached inside her purse to pull out a business card. She set in on a side table.

"Mr. Carson, I am sure it was the police who told you Phillip Nava was murdered. From what you tell me, it sounds as if you've been in contact with Leslie since then. Please, tell her I have a message from her grandfather." She paused. "I'll leave now. I want to help her. I don't bring any trouble with me."

He grunted again, and returned the binoculars to his eyes.

Johanna looked around the café and spotted Ava in the corner near the entrance to the restrooms. She slid into the chair.

"Sorry I'm late. But I had an appointment with Leslie's neighbors. They don't know where she is either . . . maybe."

The server hurriedly dropped off two cups of steaming coffee and a small bowl containing assorted sugars and cream.

"It's okay. I spent the morning with Eric's parents," Ava said. "I had to be careful. It was clear they had no word from him. They didn't know he was missing until they were interviewed by the police. I told them I had come by to check on them." She put her hands around the cup and stared into the liquid. "From our conversation it was clear they had no idea he was in any danger. Evidently, he told them we were going to Hawaii together and I was continuing on." Ava took a long sip. "They were already worried. His mom kept squeezing my hand. I told them Eric always landed on his feet and it was likely he didn't even know people were looking for him. He wasn't great at staying in touch. I told them I wouldn't leave for Australia until I knew he was safe," her voice drifted off into space.

Johanna let a silence settle between them, and then spoke. "Ava, you're right, there's a good chance Eric is off doing his Eric thing." Johanna reached across the table to cover her friend's hand. "Two weeks from now, this will be behind you. Please, how can I help?"

Ava pulled back her hand.

"Speaking of help, Johanna, are you still 'helping' Luden?" Ava said with a biting tone and air quotes.

A frown flitted across Johanna's face.

"I'm helping him to connect with his granddaughter. Why?"

"He's responsible for Eric's disappearance."

"Why would you say that?" Johanna couldn't stop her voice from rising. "You don't know it's the truth."

Ava turned away looking over her shoulder out the window. She spoke as if there was no one sitting in front of her.

"Have you asked yourself, why he sounds so earnest to find his granddaughter—now?" An unsmiling Ava turned to face Johanna. "I mean it wasn't until you approached him about Leslie contacting you that he remembered he even had a granddaughter." She leaned in. "Eric was probably looking for leads—maybe it did sound like blackmail to someone. Eric could have been overzealous, and . . . and . . . wonder if he's dead." Tears glazed her eyes.

"He's not dead, Ava. He's a survivor," Johanna said as much to herself as her friend. "I understand why you might be skeptical about Carl Luden. And it's possible that I could have been taken in by him. But he had nothing to do with Eric. Remember, Eric didn't even know how to contact Luden without searching for someone who might know him."

"Maybe so, Dean said the police can't locate Eric. It's like he's dropped off radar." Ava rubbed her forehead. "This whole thing is so convoluted with Luden and his vanishing granddaughter. It brings a whole other aspect to what's been happening. Did you ever consider that your determination to chase down your reluctant client is because you just want to cater to your ideal of being a savior . . . a . . . a knight in training, with silver armor sweeping in to save the day."

"A knight in training! I don't deserve that."

They stared at each other for a long moment and then Ava's eyes filled.

"No, you don't. I'm sorry. I'm just so worried I . . ."

"You're wrong." Johanna gave her friend a mischievous smile. "I'm already a full knight."

Ava couldn't stifle her chuckle.

CHAPTER SEVENTEEN

JOHANNA, STARTLED AT THE HAND placed on her shoulder, looked up.

"Nick!" She called out, and quickly shut down her laptop hoping he hadn't noticed her screen.

His warm brown eyes looked amused as he took the chair in front of her desk. She tried her best not to show her pleasure at seeing him.

"Hi. Marty said I could come back to your office." He nodded toward the computer. "Did I catch you at a bad time?"

"No, not at all, I was just deep in thought writing up notes. It's been a few days since we've talked."

"I plan on explaining. Can I pull you away for lunch?"

She hesitated only a moment. Work could wait, or at least be postponed for a little break.

"Yes, I'm starving." She stood and came from around her desk. "How about we go to Murray's? We can walk and I'd love a pizza."

"So would I."

They stood together and hugged.

"Hi," he said.

"Hi," she responded.

Nick gave her a squeeze and a long look. "Wow, for once my

timing must be right on." A wide grin spread across his face. "Let's not waste a minute. Let's go."

Small talk filled the next minutes. Their footsteps fell into a matching cadence as they strode down the sidewalk for the short three blocks.

"You've been busy," Johanna said. "I saw your name in the paper— the interstate fraud case?"

"Yeah, that one taught me a lot."

She bit back a response and instead "Sounds like you're enjoying your work."

"Yeah, I am. Look Johanna, I know I haven't . . ."

He stepped around a harried looking woman pushing a wheeled cart.

She held up her hand. "No explanation needed." She smiled pointing to the door. "Besides, we're here. Let's enjoy lunch."

Murray's was half-empty and the pungent smell of Parmesan coupled with seasoned tomato sauce greeted them as they entered. Nick nodded toward a red leather booth in the rear. Johanna followed.

"Ready to order?" a server appeared with flatware and napkins while they were getting settled.

"I want a mini pepperoni and sausage." Johanna said pushing the menu aside. "And, just water."

Nick nodded. "I'll have the same."

The server tucked the menus under her arms as she tapped the order into a handheld and walked to the beverage service.

Johanna turned to look Nick in the eyes.

"So detective, tell me why you *really* came to see me."

He shook his head. "I honestly thought lunch with a . . . a friend was called for." A smile hovered on his lips. "I've missed you."

"Nah, a casual visit during the day, and no beer order?" She tilted her head. "Nope, you're on duty. I agree, this is an overdue lunch, but I have no doubt you're working."

He raised his eyebrows. "Can't it be both?"

"You mean, kill two birds with one stone?" She waved her hand over the table. "As one of the birds, excuse me if I'm not excited about you squeezing me into your busy day." She didn't try to hide the slight disappointment in her own voice.

"Johanna, I—"

"I'm sorry that's not fair." She shook her head and gave him a weak smile. "Do me a favor, let's get the work agenda out of the way. What do you want to know?"

He looked down at his hands and shook his head. He opened his mouth to speak at the same time their pizza was delivered. Johanna reached over immediately and put two slices on her plate.

"Yes? What is it?"

She took a bite. Nick followed her lead.

"We understand you've been in contact with Carl Luden."

Johanna noticed it was not a question.

"Yes, I'm helping him find his granddaughter, Leslie Todd. I said I'd use my research to reunite them. But I'm not having much luck."

"Isn't that a little outside of your . . . your ancestry search skill set?"

She thoughtfully took another bite. "Have you been talking to Ava?"

"Yes, she thinks he's responsible for Eric Lowell's . . . let's say unresponsiveness." He paused, taking a sip of his water. "We want to talk to Luden and to Lowell."

"You're not alone. Ava hasn't been able to talk to, or find Eric, for the past days. He always kept in touch with her." Johanna returned his gaze. "I don't know where Luden is, Detective. He's the one that gets in touch with me—not me with him."

Slowly finishing a pizza slice, Nick dabbed his mouth with a napkin. She pushed down her mounting impatience. He leaned back in his chair.

"She told us that's what *you* think. We're not sure about the timing. Putting that aside, we have additional interests in Luden. He may be a lynch pin in other . . . activities. Lowell's disappearance is just the latest question mark."

"Maybe if you could protect him from the real bad guys, he would come forward."

"We can. I'd appreciate it if you let me know when he gets in touch with you." Nick's voice held tension. "When Luden contacts you, tell him we'll shield him . . . if he cooperates."

Johanna nodded.

"All right I will."

They fell into silence. Johanna grabbed the other pizza slice on her plate and quickly made short work of it. Nick raised his eyebrows.

"You *were* hungry."

Wiping her lips, she returned his smile. Nick reached for her hand.

"Johanna, I—"

She opened her mouth to speak, but Nick shook his head.

"No, this time let me talk." He squeezed her fingers. "I really like you and I don't want this . . . this case, or any case, to come between us. I was wrong to combine work with pleasure. Will you give me another chance to ask you out? I'll fix you dinner."

"You can cook?" It was her turn to raise her eyebrows. "All this time you never told me."

"Ah, I'm glad I still have some secrets."

"How can I refuse?"

"Good. Are you available on Saturday?"

She grinned and nodded.

Nick took out his wallet, shaking his head when Johanna reached for her purse.

"I've got to get back." He placed bills on top of the check. "At the risk of destroying a very nice lunch, there is something I want to tell you."

"This was a very nice lunch." Johanna smiled broadly. She

placed her purse straps over her shoulders. "What is it you want to tell me?"

"We know the whereabouts of Leslie Todd."

Her smile was quickly replaced with a frown.

Nick grimaced. "I guess no dinner, huh?"

TRINIDAD

TRINIDAD WAITED UNTIL MARTY HAD FINISHED his call. He glanced up to see her and held up two fingers. And in two minutes after a few words, he turned to her.

"What's up?" he avoided her eyes.

"What is up, Marty is you have stopped speaking to me since our conversation yesterday about your future."

"Nah, I'm talking to you."

"That is right. You talk to me but . . . uh . . . you do not talk *to* me." She came around to the side of the counter. "I was wrong to discourage you. If you want to be a private detective—then that is what you should try to be."

He leaned forward in his chair and clasped his hands on the edge of the desk.

"You're forgiven," he said. "Yes, I want to be a private detective. I know I can be a good one."

Trinidad gave a deep nod.

"Well then, it is settled. If I can help you or you have any questions you must ask me."

"Okay," he tilted his head. "Are you sure? Any question?"

"Any question."

"Why do you always wear black? I asked Ava and she said it was because you lost a friend. But I don't think that's it, or at least not all of it."

Trinidad's eyes widened and she took a couple of steps back.

"It is a . . . a personal question," she stuttered. "I did not . . . not mean," she faltered and saw his concern. She took a long exhale. "I

. . . I do not know anymore. It is what is inside me."

"No joy?"

She winced.

"No joy, yes, that is it," she mused, then added with a lackluster smile. "You will make a good detective, Marty."

TRINIDAD DECIDED A RESTAURANT COULD PROVIDE privacy and convenience, if not food—which was good, since so far Simone had only ordered a soft drink.

The email from the County Clerk's Office came late the day before. Trinidad had been checking her inbox every fifteen minutes until it finally appeared.

Simone's father agrees to meet. It was followed by detailed contact information and a declaration that Jonathan Kerr had approved the County to release his information to his daughter.

"I'm not too sure I'm ready, Trinidad." Simone looked down at her hands. "I know I'm the one who started things . . . but now . . .. I'm scared and nervous and my stomach is upset."

Trinidad gave her an understanding smile.

"Yes. I know but, it is likely the same for him." She patted the woman's hand. "Remember, this is for your health. He has the same condition as you. He will probably be more nervous than you."

"Maybe . . . but . . ." She hesitated. "I was wondering if you could speak with him first. Like an introduction to me. All this time . . . it's been so long . . . I . . ." her voice drifted.

"Of course, of course, Simone. I will contact your father and will meet with him first. I will try to see him tomorrow or maybe even today," Trinidad said. "But remember he responded to you. It is you he wants to meet."

Trinidad meant for her words to soothe and calm, but they had the opposite effect. Simone's jaw tightened and there was an obvious tic showing on her left eyelid.

Simone leaned across the table.

"You make it sound so easy. But, he had an affair with my mother and then abandoned us both. Now, he gets contacted by his bastard child who wants to drop some guilt-trip medical issue on him." Her words came spitting out. "He wants to meet me out of curiosity. Where has he been all these years?"

"Simone, what is the matter? Where do your words come from?" Trinidad frowned. "Why are you saying this now?"

"Because . . . because I'm a fool and sometimes reality hits me." She tapped the side of her head with the palm of her hand. All my life I thought my father was one man, and here I am, an adult, finding out I was lied to . . . and lived a lie because no one cared enough to tell me the truth. No wonder my male relationships were screwed up. Men just played on my vulnerability."

"Yes, Simone, it is quite a list of complaints you have."

"You make it sound like it's just self-pity. And, maybe it is." She swiped at her eyes with a tissue. "This morning my doctor gave me my 'blood-letting' schedule for the next six months. Did you hear that, 'blood-letting'? It sounds like I'm a vampire." Tears formed in her eyes. "Starting next Wednesday I have to go to the medical lab to have contaminated blood taken from my body—every week for the rest of my life."

Trinidad stiffened and pressed her lips together. She looked past her client out the window and then turned back.

"It does not sound pleasant and it is unfortunate you are in this place in life." She tilted her head. "But you are here. That is the way it is. I am so sorry there is nothing I can do. Why did you ever want to spend your time tracking your ancestors to find your father?"

She shrugged. "Frankly, you ask me now and I don't why I had to know. At first, I thought . . . I thought I would re-unite with my family, people who I belonged to—was a part of. And yes, I wanted to understand my condition and receive a little sympathy. Maybe find out that my father is treated with a cure. But, now, I realize finding my people—my 'loving' aunts, came with baggage and . . . and the facts in all this time my own father didn't reach out to me." She straightened. "I guess now it just makes me sad, abandoned and angry."

"You are right, there is a lot to know." Trinidad nodded. "But, you are happy that you are about to meet your father?"

"Yes, I'm happy, but there's no . . . no—"

"Joy," Trinidad murmured.

IT WAS EARLY SATURDAY MORNING. At first, Trinidad didn't realize this man with a slight bent and heading her way was Simone's father. It had taken only one attempt to reach Jonathan Kerr. He had answered his phone the day before after one only ring. He agreed immediately to meet Trinidad in a park on the Berkeley estuary. Kerr leaned heavily on his walker as he stepped slowly down the path toward the park bench. He looked nothing like she expected, until he raised his head and Simone's eyes gazed back at her.

Balancing his walker with his left hand, he reached out with his right.

"Ah, I can tell I'm not what you were expecting."

"No, I was surprised. You look so much like your daughter," Trinidad took his hand. "My name is Trinidad Owens. As I said on the phone, I am with Legacy Consultants. Simone hired me to assist her in locating you, she very much wants to know you."

He gingerly slid the walker to his left side and sat down on the other end of the bench.

"Yes, I want to explain . . . er, I need to explain to her my absence all these years. Actually I wasn't really absent, I gave the County my information. The county advocate said there was a medical issue, that Simone was sick. It's the hemochromatosis, isn't it?" He rubbed his eyebrows with his hand. "All her life I stayed away. My disease affected my life miserably. I was consumed. A child would have only complicated things more. I got through the best I could. My disease didn't show itself until after she was born. It's a long story." He shook his head.

"Do not worry, Mr. Kerr. We all have long stories. Simone will want to hear about hers."

He stared off as if he didn't hear her.

"There was always this attraction between Tanya and me," he said. "But, I was married at the time and had to lay low. To save face from being pregnant, Tanya married the first guy who asked her. He was boring, but he was there." He said quietly. "I had hoped the baby wouldn't inherit the condition. Tanya only had slight symptoms and I didn't start to evidence until, like I said, I was in my late thirties." He ran his hand through his thin hair. "I used to be a good-looking guy, but now I look terrible. It's my liver. I need a transplant, but they tell me I'll run out of time first."

Trinidad frowned. She did not want to be the one to fill the silence.

Kerr moistened his lips.

"After the divorce, for which my ex made me pay deeply—talk about Satan's spawn. But, my freedom was worth any price. You need to know her to—"

"I have met Audrey," Trinidad quickly interjected.

He showed a grim smile. "Okay, then you *do* know." He continued, "It took a while, but I put my life back together and then wham—my liver. I can't seem—"

"Mr. Kerr, I agree it sounds as if you have many injustices. I do not judge." She looked him in the eyes. "Simone has had her doctor's diagnosis and it does not look good."

"Ah, the blood-letting."

Trinidad nodded. "Yes, as I said, I represent Simone who wants to meet you and to learn about her family and the disease you share from your side."

"You're very young to be so wise. I guess I'm just feeling sorry for myself." He looked out toward the parking lot and slapped his hands against his thighs. "All right, it's far past time. I'm ready for my daughter to meet me."

"Good. As we talked, I will come back with Simone this afternoon." Trinidad stood.

TRINIDAD SENSED SIMONE'S NERVOUSNESS. It WASN'T her choice that the public park should be the gathering place for father and daughter, but Kerr had insisted as they were finishing up their meeting.

"It's best for me to stretch out my legs. I can be prone to cramps," he had said vigorously rubbing his knees.

Now, sitting silently outdoors staring at the path leading from a grove of trees Trinidad was not so sure giving Simone an opportunity to runaway was a good idea.

Simone looked like a small deer ready to dart. She took another deep breath.

"It will be all right, Simone." Trinidad patted her hand. "Do not worry. Your father is looking forward to meeting you."

Simone's glance spoke her skepticism.

"Did he actually—"

"Look, your father is here." Trinidad stood and gave a brief wave at the figure hobbling down the walkway.

Jonathan Kerr raised his cane in acknowledgement, and relatively quickly made his way to their bench. He held back a few feet and produced a flash smile.

"Hello, you look so much like your mother. But you definitely have my eyes." He held his hand out then moistened his lips and took a breath. "I guess I'm your father."

She slowly reached out her hand but then quickly pulled back. "Hello."

His hand went to his side. He rushed his words, "I . . . I understand we suffer from the same disease." Kerr sat next to his daughter. "You can see what it has done to me. The doctor's appointments alone take up most of my week and the medicine, oh my God, the medicine. You'll soon find out. They don't tell you how it affects the rest of your body. I don't know how much more I can take.

Fortunately, I have enough money to pay for a caregiver who helps my wife. I have a new wife she—"

"I . . . I . . . I have wanted this moment for so long." Simone interrupted. "Well, ever since I discovered that the man who raised me . . . who held my hand when I was sick and who came and picked me up from school when the nurse sent me home, wasn't my birth father."

Kerr frowned. "Well he didn't have my pain to come home to. I had to go from specialist to specialist. And, my hair used to be thick as carpet, now it's thin as paper."

Simone abruptly stood. Trinidad rose to stand next to her. Kerr stopped speaking, looking up a wrinkled brow indicating his confusion.

Trinidad stole a side surprised look at Simone's changed demeanor. "Simone, what—"

"I'm sorry, Trinidad. I've changed my mind." Simone peered into her father's eyes. "I wanted so much to have a family to go to, people who care about me. People who would share my past and future but this man has not once asked how I was, or how I was handling my condition, or even apologizing for ignoring my existence for almost thirty years."

"Wait, that's not fair," Kerr protested. "Your mother never wanted me in your life. And Audrey, let alone Maryanne, well they made my life hell. I came today to meet you . . . to . . . to get to know you. I do feel guilty about not looking you up, but my condition has taken away my life and keeps me—"

"Enough!" Simone yelled and grappled inside her purse. "Come on Trinidad, he doesn't care about me or my life. I'm just someone else he can complain to." She straightened her shoulders. "Goodbye, Mr. Kerr."

Trinidad nodded, taking out a tissue for the tears trickling down the woman's cheeks. Simone gave Trinidad a look of gratitude, dabbed at her eyes, and without a word turned and walked toward the parking lot.

"We will go now, Mr. Kerr," Trinidad said, holding out an envelope "Here is Simone's contact information and I will give her your contact information."

"Fine, yes of course," he said hobbling to stand. "She's upset. But she doesn't understand."

"No, that is just it, she finally does understand," Trinidad turned to follow Simone. "You never once offered to give her a hug. You never once even said her name."

AVA

AVA LOOKED DOWN AT THE SPREADSHEET on her desk. The dig team would be able to work around her absence for a couple of weeks. She glanced at her phone, still nothing from Eric. *Where was he?* She couldn't ignore the sinking feeling in her stomach that she might never see him again.

Marty appeared in her doorway.

"Ava, you have a visitor—a Paul Kennedy."

"Is he a new client?"

"No, I don't think so." Marty added, leaning into the room and whispering. "He looks like a cop, he's got a card but it doesn't say much."

He handed Ava a crisp white card.

"Put him in the conference room, I'll meet with him there."

Kennedy was tall, with medium brown skin, dark brown hair and eyes. He was good-looking and had an air of assuredness that bespoke he knew what he was doing. Ava shook his outstretched hand. She agreed with Marty. He was some branch of law enforcement.

"Ava Lowell, how can I help you, Mr. Kennedy?"

"I'm hoping you can help me locate a Carl Luden. I understand he's a client of your company."

His voice was crisp, authoritative, and yet considerate.

It immediately put Ava on guard.

"I'm sorry, can I have another business card for our files?"

"Of course." He reached into his suit's top pocket and handed her another card. "I work for the Bureau of Insurance Investigations. Some years ago, Mr. Luden was determined to be the beneficiary of a fairly large claim held by a domestic firm. However, that company went bankrupt and were bought out. We have been trying to clear their books for some time. Luden's claim is one we've been trying to close down."

"Interesting, please sit," she said, her mind working quickly. "What has led you here?"

He smiled. "We have a top notch research team. His name finally appeared on some communication links he provided for the policy. We cleared all contact info retrieved from that source, but while it wasn't enough to locate him we were able to learn from a companion source he had recently placed calls to this number."

"I see. You can trace calls?"

He didn't respond.

"I don't want to waste your time, Mrs. Lowell," he said. "Is Mr. Luden your client?"

She opened her mouth to answer but she could hear voices in the lobby then Trinidad appeared in the doorway and looked into the room.

"Ava, I must interrupt quickly. Excuse me, sir."

Ava noticed Kennedy did a restrained visual assessment of Trinidad. She also noticed Trinidad held her eyes down. Interesting.

Ava smiled. "I must apologize again, Mr. Kennedy. I will return shortly."

"Of course."

Ava led the way to the break room and shut the door.

"Trinidad, what is the matter?"

"I have seen that man before, Ava. He was outside our building at the coffee truck one or two mornings last week." She whispered. "Marty just told me that this Mr. Kennedy says he is looking for Carl Luden. This cannot be."

"Why? Our visitor says he has been looking for him for a number of years to reconcile paperwork from a defunct insurance policy."

"No, Ava. He has not been looking for Carl Luden for a number of years. Mr. Luden told Johanna he has only made up his name not long ago. This man is no friend to Carl Luden."

Paul Kennedy was gone by the time they returned to the conference room.

"I knew he wasn't what he appeared to be," Marty recounted. "He left in a hurry. Said he had to respond to an emergency and he would be back in touch."

"I am clearly out of the loop," Ava said. "Trinidad you've been working with Johanna. She knows Luden is not one of my favorite people, but I'm not ready to throw him under bus without proof."

Trinidad looked puzzled. "Ava, I do not think you are able to throw Carl Luden under the bus anyway, Marty would have to help you. But I don't understand what good would it do?"

Marty and Ava exchanged laughs. Ava explained before the frown on Trinidad's forehead deepened.

"Trini, it's an American saying. It means—"

"It means we're not giving up on the person yet," Johanna, coat in hand, had come in unnoticed to join the group.

"Exactly," Ava said, catching her eyes. "Johanna, when you get settled, we need to talk about a couple of things."

"Sure, I'll be right there."

"Ava, we have these sayings in Trinidad Tobago, also." Trinidad picked up her mail from the slot behind Marty's desk. "But *not* when the saying is longer than the meaning."

CHAPTER EIGHTEEN

JOHANNA CLOSED THE DOOR BEHIND HER and took the chair in front of Ava's desk. Her gaze took in the boxes of books lining the wall.

Instead of sitting behind her desk, Ava took the chair next to her.

"You sounded pretty serious out there, what did you want to see me about?"

"We had a visitor today," Ava responded. "He was looking for Carl Luden."

"Luden." Johanna frowned. "Why? Who was this visitor?"

"A Paul Kennedy, he lied about being some sort of insurance investigator trying to return money. I didn't believe him for a second," Ava said, giving her his card. "Trinidad smartly pointed out Luden didn't give himself that name until after he dumped the feds. Oh, by the way, I just gave Trinidad the assignment to see what she could find out about him."

"This is all such a big mess." Johanna rubbed her temples. "I had lunch with Detective Quinn on Friday he said they knew where Leslie Todd was."

"Johanna, that's great. Now we can get this whole case over with."

"Not so fast," she said. "He made it subtly clear it would be in exchange for us giving him the whereabouts of Luden."

"Subtly clear—I don't even know what that means," Ava said. "It seems like an oxymoron."

"I'm beginning to feel like an oxymoron." Johanna shook her head.

The two women gave each other a long look, and then broke out into laughter.

Ava squeezed out between chuckles, "if you are an oxymoron, then I'm a paradox."

Johanna dabbed at her eyes as the door to the office opened and Trinidad poked her head in.

"I am glad to hear so much happiness. It has been a long time since we have it here," Trinidad said with a smile. Then she held out the business card. "Ava, I think I may have found something about our visitor today."

Both women straightened. Ava turned to face her.

"What Trini?"

Trinidad took the seat behind the desk.

"I have two things to report." She said solemnly. "One, my first client is closed." She placed a sheet of paper in front of both of them. "I wrote my client notes for Marty to put in the file. Simone Griffin met her father, Jonathan Kerr. So I completed our contract, but it was not a happy meeting. He is a cold fish, she is not much better. They are actually much alike. But they will probably not be continuing on as a family.

"Trinidad, it's hard to take in sometimes that people want to know their history for a number of reasons, we don't guarantee happiness," Johanna said.

"I know. I learn something each time I finish a client." Trinidad said, closing the file folder in front of her. "I have a number two thing to report. Ava, I did as you said and researched Mr. Kennedy's information on his card. First, there is no Bureau of Insurance Investigations and second, the phone number is just a message line. But, I am not stopped. I think I know how to find out more."

"Hold just a moment, Trinidad. I think I know why our visitor came to us." Johanna clasped her hands on the desk. "I told Detective Quinn I had no idea how to get in touch with Carl Luden. That he gets in touch with me when he wants to. I'm not sure the detective believed me. Anyway, he said since Phillip Nava's murder they had been keeping a watch on our building." She raised her hand in understanding when Ava started to protest. "I know, I know, but he said they've been watching the building, not us."

"Ah, so when Mr. Luden came to our office, they thought they had him." Ava murmured.

"Yes," Johanna nodded. "Except, evidently Luden is also an expert at disguise and he somehow slipped through their fingers by changing his look on the way out."

"Then my news will be useful," Trinidad said smugly.

"Trinidad, if you could just hold off stretching out your moment of drama, I assure you it will be appreciated," Johanna said. "What is it?"

Trinidad looked miffed.

"Yes, I will continue. Mr. Kennedy is not with the insurance company, but he is with the government." Trinidad leaned over the desk. "He was driving a car with government plates."

"How did you find that out?" Ava asked. "And which government?"

Johanna noticed Trinidad's puzzled look.

"She means do you know if it was a federal car or a state car? And I want to know how you found it out too."

"Ah, well, I asked Felix from the coffee truck," Trinidad said. "He is a friend and he tells me for the past week, he sees Mr. Kennedy drive to our building in a government car." She raised an eyebrow. "There is no sign on the car. It is not labeled. So, no one will know. But it has government license plates."

Johanna and Ava exchanged looks.

"All federal plates are marked with a letter prefix," Johanna mused. "It indicates the agency to which the vehicle was assigned, for example "C" for the Department of Commerce." She faced Trinidad. "Did Felix give you the plate number?"

Trinidad reached for her phone. "He told me the license plate say US Government across the top and had numbers with an "I" in front."

Johanna and Ava said together.

"The I.R.S."

MARTY PASSED AROUND CUPS OF COFFEE. Ava huddled over her mug and Trinidad continually stirred hers. Johanna leaned back in the office chair with her eyes closed.

"What do we do now?" Marty asked.

"There are not a lot of options," Ava spoke. "We have to tell Kennedy what we know." She nudged her partner. "Right, Johanna? We will tell him, right?"

"We have two clients," Johanna edged away from the nudge and looked around the room. "We have to let Leslie Todd and Carl Luden know we've been approached by . . . by government officials."

Trinidad shook her head. "First, Johanna, you say Leslie Todd but we don't know where she is. And, Carl Luden is maybe a criminal, so we do not owe him any . . . any faith."

"That's right, Trinidad, *maybe* a criminal is a good point. Luden is in a protection program for a reason. A program that appears to have failed him. I'm not going to betray him. So we should give him a chance to go forward to law enforcement on his own." Johanna retorted. "And I plan on contacting Detective Quinn about speaking to Leslie Todd since she's already been talking to the police."

"Good grief, Johanna, what is it with you and this guy, Luden? Why do you even want to trust him? How do you know that the protection program slipped his identity?" Ava said not hiding the amazement in her voice. "And I can tell you Nick Quinn is not going to help you contact Leslie Todd unless you give up Carl Luden."

The two women studied each other with annoyance.

Marty cleared his throat. "Want to know what I think?"

The three women turned to look at him.

Trinidad tilted her head. "What, Marty, what do you think?"

He straightened against the wall.

"I think we're being dragged into the middle of a game, and we don't know the rules." Marty took a sip from his cup. He held up his hand. "Bear with me on this. Luden was betrayed or thought he was going to be betrayed by the feds protection team—so he goes underground on his own."

There were affirming nods and he continued.

"He hides out in Napa below the federal radar. It's clear he's still afraid of those he flipped on. Maybe he senses they are closing in on him. Still, he keeps track of his family. His daughter dies, and he can't reappear. He always wanted to connect with his granddaughter, but for her own safety—and his, he stays away, until coincidentally she reaches out to him first." He stopped with a frown. "Only now we know it didn't turn out well, and involved a dead body. And up until Leslie tracked him through us, he was doing okay."

"That's right again," Johanna said. "We led Leslie to Carl Luden and she must have told Nava we had his location. Nava got there first, something went wrong and Nava got killed by someone who wanted to frame Luden."

No one looked convinced.

"That's all true, we may have gotten this ball started," Marty rushed. "But, I also think there's some reason why Luden is all of a sudden interested in reuniting with his granddaughter. Why now?"

"Do you think Luden would kill Nava, his granddaughter's fiancé?" Johanna asked.

"Do you?" Marty pushed back.

Johanna puckered her brow and shook her head. "I don't know."

"And Eric?" Ava interjected. "What about him?"

Johanna was silent.

Trinidad came from behind Ava's desk and sat on its edge.

She pointed in the air with her pen. "It seems to me that—"

"Enough." Johanna stood. "No more of this brainstorming session. I need more real information. We have serious work. This could affect Legacy's reputation. I'm going to get a few answers."

She could feel their concern as the door clicked behind her.

TRINIDAD

EARLY THE NEXT MORNING, STANDING AT THE END of the coffee truck line, Trinidad looked down at her watch when she caught the motioning nod from Felix, the signal they had agreed to the evening before.

Right on time.

She strode up to the car parked in the red zone and tapped on the passenger side window. It slowly rolled down.

"Can I help you Ma'am?"

"Yes, you can. I would like to speak to Paul Kennedy. The card he gave me doesn't work. I think you know him." Trinidad showed him the business card and pointed to the rear of the car. "You have an 'I' on your plates."

The gray-haired man frowned. "Can I have your name Ma'am?" He took a small pad of paper out of his shirt pocket.

"Yes, my name is Trinidad Owens, I work for Legacy Consultants." She turned and pointed. "I work in the building you are watching. Mr. Kennedy came to our office yesterday looking for . . . for someone. I do not mean to bother you. Can you give me a number for him that works?"

"Ma'am, I can't help you. I'm just a public servant here on a coffee break. I don't know who you're talking about. But, why don't you give me your phone number?"

"My phone number why?" Trinidad backed away. "If you are a public servant, can I have your phone number?"

Before he could respond, his phone rang and pointing it out to Trinidad, he put the window up.

Crossing her arms and determined to wait, Trinidad caught a movement out of the corner of her eye. Felix was waving his arms at her. She frowned and took a few steps toward the coffee truck before feeling a tap on her shoulder. She whirled around.

"Sorry, didn't mean to startle you, Ms. Owens," Paul Kennedy said looking amused and not sounding at all apologetic. "I understand you're looking for me?"

TRINIDAD DELIBERATELY CHOSE THE SMALL LUNCHROOM café on the corner when she turned down Kennedy's suggestion to talk back at the office.

"I want to talk with you first," she said. "The office is not good right now, too much counterversary."

"Controversy?" he asked.

Trinidad gazed up to the sky. "That is what I say. Now, we can talk here about what you are really here about. You are not from an insurance company. You drive a government car and you have friends who also drive government cars. We think you are with the FBI."

His disarming smile caught her off guard.

"You're right Ms. Owens." He reached into his pocket and taking out a card placed it in front of her. "This is my office card."

She picked it up and read out loud, "Special Investigations, Paul Kennedy." She looked him in the eyes. "But it does not say who you are investigating for."

"That's right." He leaned against the car and crossed his arms. "Very quick of you to notice."

Trinidad ran her hand over her hair pulled tight into a pony tail.

"ERS?" she pronounced, raising the card. "What department is that?"

Kennedy broke into a hearty laugh and the nearby patrons turned to look.

"You are charming." He grinned, and then quickly his face turned stern. "It's I.R.S. It stands for the Internal Revenue Service. We handle the collection and enforcement of tax monies for the United States."

"So, you told us a lie about the insurance company to get information. In my country the Police Services have the respect of the people, they do not have to lie."

"I did not lie. I'm in the collection recovery section of the I.R.S., and I'm sure Trinidad-Tobago security forces are excellent in many ways but—"

"How do you know my country?"

"It's my job to know." Kennedy smiled and glanced at the parking lot activity. "Ms. Owens, as much as I understand and appreciate your reluctance to be open with me, we are running out of time." He stood. "I think it best to return with you to your office so I can speak with everyone."

CHAPTER NINETEEN

J OHANNA SAW MARTY'S EYES WIDENED and she turned to see who had entered the lobby.

Trinidad was walking in front of Paul Kennedy and trying to signal a message with her eyes, but Johanna was not able to interpret.

"Mr. Kennedy, I presume," she said, holding out her hand. "I missed meeting you yesterday. I understand you're following up on an insurance claim and—"

"No, Johanna, he already knows we know he is not with insurance," Trinidad said. "I . . . I found him this morning still watching our building."

Marty picked up a ringing phone. It was clear he was also trying to listen to the conversation in front of him as he responded to the caller in a muffled voice.

"Perhaps if we could meet in your office, Mrs. Hudson?" Kennedy said.

Johanna noticed his use of her name.

"Of course. Trinidad can you let Ava know we'll have our staff meeting later this afternoon?"

Ignoring Trinidad's raised eyebrows, Johanna gestured for Kennedy to follow her down the hall. Entering her office, she directed him to the chair in front of her desk. She took the chair next to him.

"Mr. Kennedy, it is my understanding you are trying to locate a Carl Luden."

"We don't try, Ms. Hudson. We *will* locate Carl Luden," he replied in a no-nonsense tone. "What I need to know is if you are sheltering him?"

"Sheltering him! No, not at all . . . I . . .," she stumbled to find the right words. "I came across Carl Luden trying to serve a client contract for an ancestry search. That's it."

"So this has nothing to do with your husband?"

Johanna's heart beat began pounding in her ears. She could see Kennedy's lips moving but the sound of his words were smothered. She slid her trembling hand under her thigh.

Her husband, Joel Hudson, and their two-year old daughter, Amber, had been killed in an auto accident three years before. It was much later she found Joel was an undercover operative for the FBI.

"Mrs. Hudson?"

She realized this was not the first time he had said her name.

"Yes, I'm sorry. What was your question?

"Your husband's work made him privy to cases that could have brought him into contact with John Ackerman," Kennedy paused as if to see her reaction. "Ackerman was—"

"I'm familiar with the name," she cut him off.

She had remembered all the names in the boxes Joel had left behind in the basement before the FBI had carted them away. She had spent days going through his papers and files struggling to find a reason for why her family had been killed.

"Really, you know the name?"

"Bear with me, I have a question for you." Johanna moistened her lips. "What has Ackerman to do with Carl Luden?"

Kennedy glanced at his phone.

"Mrs. Hudson, Carl Luden is a person of interest. We need to speak with him to clarify some . . . issues," he said. "This is not a request. If you know where he is you must tell us."

"But I don't know where he is," she heard her voice rise. "He contacts me whenever he's ready. I'm only helping him find his granddaughter, Leslie Todd."

"He wants to meet with Leslie Todd?"

"Yes, she's disappeared," Johanna frowned. "Luden wants to find her. It didn't start out that way. She first came to me looking for her grandfather, nothing more. It was after that when Carl Luden decided now he wanted to meet her. But, after the Nava murder she has not responded to my calls or texts." She gestured toward the door. "I don't know any facts. You need to speak with Detective Nick Quinn, he—"

"I know Detective Quinn."

"Of course you would," she rushed. "Well, you need to ask him about Leslie Todd. He told me his department knows where she is."

Kennedy was silent and gave Johanna a long look.

"So, you're trying to tell me your only interest in this is to connect a granddaughter with her grandfather? Seems a bit of walk from doing ancestry research, especially given the murder of Phillip Nava."

She didn't know why, but her words were catching in her throat. She nodded, "Yes, that's all our involvement."

"But you can see where we're coming from, Mrs. Hudson? You're the only one who's seen and talked with Luden since the killing."

"Luden told me he was in a protection program. That's not a crime. I guess, I flashed back to my life with my husband, Joel. He had us in sort of a protection program too . . . and . . . and I didn't know it. He was trying to . . . to keep us safe by not telling us about his job." She ran her hand through her hair.

"So, this affiliation you have for Luden is . . .?"

"You sound like my partner, Ava," she said. "I don't have an 'affiliation' for Carl Luden." She raised her hands in air quotes.

"Leslie, hired us to locate her grandfather. I guess Legacy was a cheap alternative to lawyers. Then after the nightmare in Napa, Luden came to me wanting to find his granddaughter. Is that so odd? I just wanted to help . . . I knew how it felt, my own daughter . . ."

She paused rubbing both her temples with shaking hands.

"You okay, Mrs. Hudson?"

"What?" She put her hands in her lap. "Yes, I'm fine."

"Mrs. Hudson, this has been a good talk. I think we have an understanding." He stood. "I'm going to leave now. I know we can count on you to let us know if Luden makes contact again."

"Yes, of course." She didn't raise her head.

"And, if you could pass the word on to the rest of your office."

IT ONLY TOOK JOHANNA A FEW MINUTES to recount the gist of Kennedy's visit to her colleagues who were huddled over the reception counter.

"That was it? He just wants us to report to him if Luden shows up again?" Marty said.

"Oh, and he left new cards." Johanna passed them around. "These have his correct information"

Ava looked down at the card, and then met Johanna's eyes. "I need sustenance. We can go for lunch and I can tell you about the news I received about the dig."

"I come too," Trinidad said. "I'm starving."

"Trini, how about I bring you back a sandwich?" Ava offered. "It would be great if you could check out Mr. Kennedy's card. We don't want him to fool us again."

Trinidad frowned. "I guess I could make sure. Or, you could just have lunch without me."

CHAPTER TWENTY

"**I** KNOW I SAID WE'D GO FOR lunch, but I need to get a few things for the trip and I have paperwork to drop off at the university," Ava spoke as she pulled out of driveway onto the busy roadway.

"Good." Johanna clicked on her seat belt. "We can talk. I'm feeling we haven't been communicating as well as we should." She turned slightly. "Ava, I haven't taken the time to tell you I'm sorry about Eric. I am hoping he is all right. I know . . . I know it must be hard."

At the corner, Johanna quenched her eyes closed at the more red than yellow light intersection as they accelerated through. She'd forgotten what a terrible driver Ava was.

"What makes it harder, Johanna is that I think you know where Luden is," Ava said, cutting in front of a car to get onto the freeway. She gave a quick side glance at her passenger. "Do you?"

"Ava, I don't know where he is any more than you do." She stared out the passenger window.

"But you have an idea."

Johanna winced as Ava's last minute lane change generated a horn blast.

"No, I don't. Can we go to Far and Away for lunch? It's at the next exit." Johanna pointed. "I'll treat, if you get us there alive."

"Done."

Far and Away was a local Asian casual restaurant hangout. The midday customers were mostly take-out, and a few tables inside were still available. They both chose large fragrant bowls of Wor Won Ton Soup and took them to a table far away from the entry.

"Well?" Ava insisted, after first taking a spoonful. "I got you here alive—talk."

Johanna nodded after taking a bite of her own steaming won ton dumpling. She continued, "Okay, the few times I've seen Carl Luden he was in some type of uniform. A working class outfit that he likely thought would help him blend in and avoid standing out in any one person's memory." She leaned in. "I questioned Thomas, our lobby security guard, I saw him actually speaking with Luden who offered to take his place while he check out his car. Which was a ruse. But Thomas said he sees so many people every day there was nothing special about Luden that caught his attention."

Ava slid her empty bowl to the edge of the table to be picked up.

"Just so you know, I got clearance from the police. I'm no longer a suspect. If I keep to my Australia schedule, I'm gone after next Tuesday. I won't be able to help you." Ava's face reflected her concern. "What's your follow-up plan?"

"Don't worry, Ava." She patted her friend's hand. "One thing that's clear is Luden seems to always know what I'm doing. I think he checks in with me when he thinks I'm coming into information he wants access to." She took out her phone to look at the time. "I'm going to ask Nick to ask Leslie Todd if I can contact her, or have her contact me. I'm meeting him in an hour. I'm hoping he'll be willing to approach her about seeing me, or at least to find out why she's avoiding me. "

"And if you two meet?"

"Then I'll let her know her grandfather wants to see her so they can mend their relationship."

"And if she has no interest in a family reunion?"

Johanna shrugged. "Then I did what I could. I no longer have a client."

THE LUNCH PATIO OUTSIDE THE POLICE DEPARTMENT was well-planned with scattered small pods of tables with seating for four. Either patio umbrellas or well-placed maples made for pleasant cover on sun filled days.

Johanna knew Nick was aware of the attempt on both their sides to avoid an awkward silence. She took a sip of her lemonade to clear her throat.

"Have you given thought to my request?"

"I wouldn't be here if I wasn't willing to talk," his voice was curt. He looked down at the small notebook he pulled from inside his coat pocket. "Before we move on, it shouldn't be a surprise we're going to need your testimony when the time comes for trial. I know you gave a statement but—"

"I know all that." She said. "Nick, what's wrong?"

He avoided her eyes. "What do you mean?"

"Why are we speaking like we're strangers? Why do I feel like I need to be on the defensive? Why do you sound the same?"

He tossed his pen on the table and leaned forward after looking over his shoulder. His jaw tightened visibly.

"How long have we known each other? A year, almost two years?" he asked. "In that stretch how many times have our interactions involved you in some kind of trouble?" He raised his hand. "Don't answer, I'll tell you—too many."

"Nick, what—"

"No, let me finish. You asked me several questions and I'm giving you my response."

She nodded for him to go ahead.

"I like you, Johanna." This time his eyes looked deep into hers. "I really like and respect you. I don't want to wonder what you're up to because it means I can't concentrate on my job. You get these notions into your head about helping people, whether they deserve you or not—whether it's safe or not. And you're off and running. It makes me crazy."

Johanna looked down at her clasped hands, and opened her mouth to speak.

"No, wait," Nick said. "I'm almost finished. Let me finish." He straightened and cleared his throat. "The Department needs your help. We need to know we can count on you to work with us. It's clear Luden feels comfortable with you. He trusts you. We want to . . . to exploit his trust."

She started to respond, but stayed quiet.

Nick paused. He deliberately avoided her stare, and instead looked off at a group of uniformed officers taking seats at a nearby table.

"He's dirty, Johanna. I know you don't want to believe it. I know you think your gut is telling you he's a good guy at heart but he isn't. He's scum." Nick turned to look at her. "And now I'm afraid you won't believe me, and this time you'll get into trouble you can't get out of and I won't be there to help you."

"I know how that feels," Johanna said quietly. "I worry about you, too."

He shook his head and pushed the slim folder he'd brought with him toward her.

"Read this. I can't let you take it with you. But, you can sit here and go through it. When you finish give me a call. I'll have my phone on me. If you agree to work with us, I have the contact information for Leslie Todd in an envelope with your name on it," Nick said. "Actually, I just spoke with her. She is going to get in touch with you, *if* we say it's safe. Ms. Todd is unsure of her feelings for her grandfather. She ran away from the Napa scene out of fear. Once she could see you were okay, she's been staying with a friend. Regardless, we tracked her down as a potential suspect in Nava's murder. Yesterday we were able to dismiss her. She knows you have been in contact with her grandfather. But she doesn't know we have our own reasons to locate Luden. We would prefer it that way."

"All right, we'll do things your way." Johanna took a long breath reaching for the file. "You seem to have thought of everything. I take it if I don't agree to work with you, I have to wait for Leslie to contact me?"

He gave a slow nod of his head. "Yep."

IT HADN'T TAKEN HER LONG TO READ THROUGH the dozen or so pages. They told the laborious story of how the feds had tracked the once-protected witness, Kevin Post, to the new identity, Carl Luden. He had changed his name twice more before landing on Luden. But it was the eventual trail of money made up of marked bills they knew he still had on him when he rolled over on his friends had caught their eye. According to the agents, he was funding crimes of money laundering. Apparently, Luden had thought enough time had passed that he could start carefully spending the money intended to protect his earlier identity.

Most of the remaining pages were copies of court depositions taken from various individuals over the past seven years. They provided background on how Luden had used his insider information to gain access to the witness protection program. But it was the name on the final deposition brought a chill to her chest. Her right hand began the familiar quiver.

John Ackerman

She frowned. Most of the document had been redacted with what looked like a broad black sharpie pen. She read slowly her blood rushing loudly in her ears. Luden knew Ackerman.

Ackerman was identified as a conspirator in the killing of her husband and daughter.

THE PAGES DROPPED FROM JOHANNA'S HAND and onto the picnic table top. She felt tears stream down her face. They kept coming and she didn't try to stop them. She didn't know how many minutes had passed. Finally, the tears stopped, but her face was still damp, and her heart seemed weighted down with grief. When she looked around, the patio tables were empty and Nick was walking toward her.

"You okay?" he asked, taking the across from her. "I know how seeing Ackerman's name could send you back to . . . to terrible times."

"Is he still in jail?"

"Yes. He's not going anywhere for another eighteen years."

"You asked if I'm okay," she said. "I'm not okay, but I am ready to work with you to nail Luden." She slid the folder over. "Tell Leslie I'm waiting for her call."

TRINIDAD

TRINIDAD DID NOT EXPECT PAUL KENNEDY would be available to see her and that she could walk into a federal building and talk with a humorless receptionist who barely acknowledged her. But, when she gave her name, Kennedy appeared before she could take a seat.

"Mr. Kennedy, I thought you said you worked for the tax department."

"I do. We are working this investigation with the FBI. We have mutual interests."

She walked behind him now, his long strides to her shorter, faster ones, as they made their way to a visitor's room.

"Is there a reason, Ms. Owens, why you didn't approach me this morning when I was in your offices?" Kennedy had taken a swivel chair, and he was making slight side to side turns.

"Yes, I did not want the others to know." She chewed her bottom lip. "Everyone is worried about Johanna. She has never gotten over the death of her husband and child. She . . . she is not herself now. She sees Carl Luden and his granddaughter as the same as her husband and daughter. She wants to protect him because she could not protect her own family." She raised her hands. "I know it is crazy but that is where we are."

"I see. What did you not want the others to know?"

"I think I know where Carl Luden is hiding."

Kennedy stopped swiveling.

"Where is he?"

"Well, maybe not where he is hiding, but how he is hiding."

"I don't understand. What do you mean 'how' he is hiding?"

Trinidad took a deep breath.

"I only see Carl Luden two times. Each time he is wearing work clothes—uniforms."

Kennedy took out his phone and placed it between them.

"I'm recording you, so I don't miss something." He also took out a pad and pen and made an entry. "What kind of uniform?"

"They were both blue with dark pants, but they were not the same. The first time he had a sweater with a label and the second time he was wearing a thick cloth jacket with a zipper up the front, but no label." She raised her voice and leaned toward the recorder. "I think he is working or pretending to work at different companies—maybe security."

"Why security?"

"Because Johanna said he took Thomas' place at our reception desk. I think he had to be wearing a uniform that looked like Thomas'. When I saw him, the uniforms could have been the same company, just not alike."

Kennedy scribbled a note.

"Miss Owens, this is helpful. You're quite the detective. We'll start checking security firms. Do you think you could describe his disguises or recognize him again?"

Trinidad frowned. "Maybe, but each time he looked different in the face. I do not think I ever saw what he really looks like. I will tell you his disguises are very good. They do not look like disguises."

Paul Kennedy put away his phone. "If they are so good, how do you know they are disguises?"

"My cousin is a member of a community theater in Fresno. He is a perfectionist and plays very seriously the roles he is given." Trinidad gave a small smile. "He says the perfect undercover disguise is one where if two people were to meet that person, and later describe them, every detail would be wrong."

"I see. Ms. Owens, if you even think you spot Luden, call me at this number." He said reaching into his pocket and handing the card out.

Trinidad glanced down. "This is no surprise, another card and another number. How many cards do you have?"

Kennedy laughed. "Way too many, but seriously this is my private number. You can call it at any time. Remember don't approach him. Just call me."

Trinidad nodded. She was glad her blush wasn't evident.

"Where did you disappear to?" Marty asked peering over the reception counter. "Ava never came back from lunch, Johanna came back from lunch but zipped out of here in a rush. And you didn't even say goodbye." He closed his laptop. "What's up?"

Trinidad sat in a lobby chair and stretched out her legs.

"Ah, Marty those criminology classes you are taking are sharpening your detective skills. I was following up on a case."

"Hmm, you have a case huh? Well I detect this; you're wearing a very pretty rose colored blouse. Is it your birthday or something?" He scrutinized her. "You know you should wear color more often. Did you go on a job interview?"

"No! Of course not, I like it here."

"Then it must be a guy."

CHAPTER TWENTY-ONE

JOHANNA ZIPPED HER PUFFER JACKET CLOSED. Her knit cap and scarf gave her extra insulation to keep away the penetrating morning chill coming off the bay. The Palace of Fine Arts was one of her favorite vistas of the Golden Gate Bridge. It was also known for its sense of old San Francisco history and its lure of beaux arts. And, all things considered, it was a great place to have a private conversation.

Leslie Todd was quick to apologize for her disappearing act. They decided to meet the next day. Leslie had chosen the location.

"Sure," Johanna replied. "The Palace is fine."

They had settled on meeting at the west side of the rotunda at the end of the lagoon next to the bordering colonnades. Johanna stared out over the water. She was grateful to find a vacant concrete bench in the sun. It was easy to spot the tourists out this morning. They weren't prepared for the weather and hurried through the open space, unlike the Bay Area natives who sauntered along, well-bundled and taking in the beauty of the site.

"Johanna?"

Johanna jerked, and turned around. Leslie was wearing sunglasses and a 49er cap. Her blonde hair grazed the top of her moss green hooded parka. She carried a modest looking camera around her neck.

"Leslie, hello," she said, holding out her hand. "I was expecting to see you come from the direction of the parking lot." She bent over to see around her visitor.

Leslie chuckled. "I like to give my fed surveillance team a run for their money. I came through those hedges over there from the street side." She nodded toward what appeared to be a thick wall of greenery. She grinned. "They'll be showing up soon."

"You're being watched by the feds?"

"Ah yes, my new best friends since the . . . the incident in Napa. Once they figured out who my grandfather was . . . well let's say I'm a person of interest to a person of interest." She gestured. "Thanks, for meeting me here. "I have a photography class nearby in the Marina district. "I can give you an amount of time without having to keep checking the clock."

Johanna looked appreciatively at the speaker. "Good for you. One of the reasons I chose this bench was because no one could get close enough to hear us. Have a seat."

Leslie settled her bags and took off her sunglasses.

"I'm sorry for abandoning you like that," she said. "I just couldn't handle dealing with the police, the disappearance of my grandfather and the fact I'd involved you and you could have been killed."

"And the fact I had tripped over your boyfriend's dead body." Johanna didn't try to hide her sarcasm.

"Yes, of course," Leslie murmured. "Johanna, Phillip and I have not been together for almost three years. I haven't seen him for almost two of those years. Ours was not a match made in heaven."

"I understand from your grandfather Phillip Nava was not high on his people's choice list either."

"I didn't know Phillip even knew I had a grandfather until after we were married and gradually he made it clear it was my grandfather he was interested in—I was just a token on his chess board." She paused. "I understand you are in contact with my grandfather. He told you he wants to meet me?"

"Yes, he does but he wants it done privately. I don't think he would care for your fed friends. He's hiding from something, but I don't know what."

Leslie turned silent and looked out over the lagoon.

"Johanna, do you know why I chose to contact Legacy? Because for me, this is a big deal. I read about what you did last year for the family in Marin and I felt you could handle my search as well as my secrets—even if I didn't know what they were myself."

"Thank you for the confidence. I still think we can help you. Witness Protection has its challenges but we can still make inroads."

"Where's my grandfather?"

"Leslie, I'm going to be honest with you. I don't know where your grandfather is. He gets in contact with me when he's ready. But he does seem to know what is going on with me. You both seem to want to meet each other, so this is a good thing. In fact, he could be looking at us now."

They both looked around and fell back into silence.

"Johanna, all I know of my grandfather is what I heard from my mother. She wanted me to never be afraid like she was growing up. She told me what it was like as a child to move in the darkness of the night with all her toys and clothes on a train from Chicago to Colorado. Her parents, my grandfather, instilled in her that a slip of the tongue could mean the breakup of the family and she could be taken away."

"Wow, that's a lot for a child to hear."

"Then they kept moving. They lived in Colorado for less than a year. She found out when they got new identities they moved to Nevada, which is where she grew up. She doesn't remember her birth name, but her last name was 'Post' in Colorado. Then her parents, my grandfather, changed their name to Todd in Nevada."

Johanna shook her head in amazement.

"It must have been a confusing and complicated way to live," she said. "Leslie, do you know why Philip Nava was killed?"

Leslie frowned through the tears that were already sliding down her cheeks.

"Philip was not a good man. At first I thought he was trying to protect me the best he could. He said when we married he didn't want me to take his name. He had some bad debts and he didn't want them to come after me." She swiped at her cheek with her fingers. "I know, it sounds idiotic to me too—now, but I was so blinded. However, I can tell you, it was always about the money."

Johanna handed her a tissue. "What money?"

"Don't worry, I already told the feds."

She accepted a packet of tissues from Johanna with a thank you smile and continued, "My grandmother set up a trust fund for my mother before my grandfather went into witness protection. It was quite . . . substantial. The feds let it stand to get my grandfather's cooperation. When my mother died, I inherited the proceeds."

"Is it possible your grandfather killed your fiancé? Did Phillip know Carl Luden was your grandfather?"

"Those are the same questions the feds asked me. Are you working for them too?"

Johanna felt herself redden.

"I won't lie to you, they have asked me to . . . to pass on any pertinent information about your grandfather. But your grandfather hired us to locate you. Our service includes client confidentiality . . . well, to the extent under the law."

"Detective Quinn said you're a forensic genealogist; that you find people who are criminals. Is my grandfather a criminal?"

Johanna looked away as a family of tourists walked past taking pictures of multiple poses against the cultural backdrop. She was surprised at Nick's labeling of her title role. She liked the sound of it.

She looked into Leslie's eyes.

"A forensic genealogist takes on clients or cases requiring ancestral research has legal implications: heir location, paternity, things like that. Such research may, or may not, arise or even lead to a crime." She reached for Leslie's hand. "Look, right now all I need to know is if you are willing to meet with your grandfather. It is not my role or within my capability to determine if he is a criminal. Your grandfather wants to see you. I am working to reunite him with you—that's it."

Johanna felt a twinge of guilt for not disclosing her expanded motivation for aiding law enforcement, but had no regrets. She would make sure no harm came to Leslie.

"Let me think on it, Johanna," the young woman said. "There's a lot going on and frankly I'm not even sure I want to meet my grandfather anymore." She frowned. "Except, it feels like it's the last thing I need to do, so I can move on with my life."

JOHANNA SAT IN HER CHAIR STARING out the window.

"How did it go?" Ava asked, offering Johanna a steaming cup of aromatic coffee as she clutched her own in her other hand.

The office was quiet. Trinidad and Marty joined them and they all gathered around the conference room table.

Johanna accepted the cup gratefully. She was still feeling the chilly fog filling her jacket from her meeting in San Francisco.

"Leslie is reluctantly willing to meet with Carl Luden. Now I just wait for him to reach out to me."

Ava gave her a curious look.

"Your tone seems to have changed. Did she raise doubts about Luden too?"

"My concerns were always raised." Johanna turned away from Ava's gaze. "I was always willing to give him the benefit of the doubt until shown otherwise."

"And now?"

"You were right, Ava. I think Carl Luden is dirty. Is that what you want to hear?"

Her friend placed her hand on her shoulder.

"No, Johanna, it's not what I want to hear," Ava said. "I'm going away next Monday and I want to know sanity will prevail while I'm gone." She paused. "With running the risk of overstating the obvious—you're working with the police, right?"

Johanna nodded.

"We are all working with the police," Trinidad interjected. "I have an idea. I think I should watch Leslie Todd steps."

"You mean follow Leslie Todd?" Marty said.

"Yes, Marty, I will use your words. I think I should follow Leslie Todd."

"Why, Trini?" Ava asked.

"I have been thinking. Who is our client?" Trinidad pulled her hair back. "What if Carl Luden contacts her on his own. Wonder if he does not want to need us anymore."

JOHANNA FELT HIS PRESENCE EVEN WITHOUT turning around in the valet line waiting for her car to be brought around.

"We need to talk," Luden said, standing close behind her.

She gave him a quick glance. He was wearing a bright orange vest over a tan jumpsuit.

"I agree. When?"

"Make it in an hour. I'll meet you at the DMV on Jackson in Hayward."

"The DMV," she responded. "Are you kidding me, why the—"

He was gone.

JOHANNA HAD TO SCRAMBLE IN BAY AREA TRAFFIC to make it to Hayward. On hands-free she called into the office and told Marty she would be late getting back.

"That's okay. I'll wait," he said.

"Marty, there's no need. Go home. Don't you have a class tonight?"

"No, school is on break. Besides, I can study here."

Johanna thought a moment. "Wait a minute. Are you guys making up some kind of 'guard Johanna' detail? Trinidad is following me and Leslie and now you're acting as my watchdog."

She quickly turned into a parking space in the last row. The DMV lot, as usual, was almost full.

"Look, Johanna, humor us will you? I've got Trini breathing down my neck and Ava looking like a boxed-in squirrel. Please, just let us do our thing, and we'll let you do yours."

She was too stressed to argue.

Johanna hurried to the DMV's glass double doors entrance and waited as Marty finished recounting the new phone messages. Moments later, stepping through the entry doors, she looked up into the face of Carl Luden, still dressed as a workman. He paused to hold the door open for her and the few people who entered alongside.

"Marty, we'll talk later—go to lunch." She spoke quickly. "Gotta' go."

Luden motioned with his head. "Let's go in, shall we?"

She tucked away her phone.

"I never would have thought the DMV was a good place to have our conversation," Johanna said, keeping stride with his long steps.

"Exactly," Luden replied heading straight for a line of vacant plastic chairs in the middle of the last row against a long wall. Johanna had to admit it wasn't likely any of the other patrons would choose to sit near their inconvenient location.

"So, Johanna, did you speak with Leslie? What did she say?"

She swallowed, she was comfortable lying, but not when so much was at stake. Luden peered at her as if he could see right through to her intent. She looked him in the eyes.

"I spoke with Leslie, she was a little cautious after the Napa nightmare, but she wants to meet you as long as I come with her."

A mixture of truth and storytelling was more convincing.

"I see, only if you come with her, interesting. Well, that won't be a problem," he said looking out over the room. "I'll get in touch with you with the details. I still have . . . partners who are very impatient and need tight control. After they are settled, I'll be leaving, this time for good. I just want to see Leslie as she is now, a grown woman, before . . . I go. I trust you, Johanna. I don't think you would betray me."

"Thank you for the trust," she said. "Carl, I have to ask. Leslie is going to want to know. Did you kill Phillip Nava?"

He squinted as if looking at the electronic "Now Serving" sign hanging over the service counter. Then he ran his tongue on the inside of his cheek.

"Are you wearing a wire, Johanna?"

Her heart beat in her ears. "No, of course not. I . . . I'm just anticipating Leslie's questions. You don't have to tell me, but she'll be asking you."

"Like I said, I want to trust you. Excuse me, but I have to go pick up my forms."

He stood, pulled a number stub out of his vest and walked toward a booth in the far corner. He returned with several sheets of paper.

"You really had to come to the DMV?" She said incredulous.

"I have found hiding in plain sight is always the best tactic. It would look odd if I sat here without pulling a number or talking to a clerk, people might remember me—us. Now we fit in with privacy and anonymity." He paused. "Johanna, I don't think I have to remind you my life has already been turned upside down. Still, I mean no one deliberate harm. I just want to meet my granddaughter before I disappear into her past."

"Yes, I understand. I—"

"I hope you do." He glanced at his phone. "Now, I have to go. I'll be contacting you soon."

"Can I have your contact number to make sure there won't be any mix-ups?"

He grinned. "Can I have Leslie's contact number?" He smiled at her awkwardness. "No, I didn't think so. We'll keep our contact as in-person only. Don't worry, I'll be in touch soon."

WHILE JOHANNA WAITED FOR NICK in an agency interview room, she checked her emails on her phone. It had been a very long and eventful day. She was exhausted and feeling stressed. He had

insisted she come to the station in the afternoon and recount what
had happened at her meeting with Leslie, and now she could also
report her surprise drop-in visit from Luden.

Nick texted her: *I need another fifteen minutes.*

Sighing and closing her eyes, she leaned back in her chair. What
exactly would she say? Leslie Todd's response to Johanna's news
was cool, almost matter-of-fact aloof. Then there was the nagging
question that had remained in the back of her mind—why now?
Why the family reunion search now, for either one of them?

Her phone buzzed and she picked it up.

"Hi Mom," she said. "I'm getting ready to go into a meeting.
Can I call you back?"

"This is real quick. I want you to come over for dinner tonight,
6 p.m.," Elisabeth Girrard rushed. "We haven't gotten together in
a long time."

"Mom, I really can't. There's—"

"Johanna . . ."

"Yes, all right, 6 p.m."

"EVERYTHING OKAY?" A TIRED LOOKING NICK slid into the chair
across from her.

"Yes, my mother is confirming our dinner date." She tucked the
phone away. "There's a lot going on."

"Why don't we start with the interactions you had *today*?"

Johanna spent the next twenty minutes explaining her conversations with Todd and Luden. Nick let her speak and said nothing.

"That's it," she said with a deep exhale.

"Okay, now let's go over it again, only slower this time. I have a
couple of questions."

It was all she could do to appear alert, and she took another
exhale she finished her tale.

"You said Leslie knows she's being followed, did it upset her?"

"No, not at all, as a matter of fact, it seemed like she enjoyed
giving them a run for their money. She called them her 'tag team.'"

Nick was silent, then, "Johanna, how did she answer your questions about Nava?"

"She didn't. If anything, she became more . . . wary with me. She was aware you and I are working together. It may have made her cautious." She rubbed her forehead. "You know, she talked about her life as a protected family member, but there was something off putting about her recitation."

"What do you mean?"

"It sounded like a recitation." Johanna leaned forward. "She was pretty much unemotional about her fiancé's death, and the only time she was even slightly animated was when she mentioned the money."

"What money?"

"I don't know. She said she'd already told the Feds about it."

Nick stared through her. Judging from his knowing expression, Johanna got the feeling Leslie had her own secrets.

Nick made hurried notes on his pad.

"All right, now go over your conversation with Luden."

Johanna was tempted to make a mock salute, but she didn't think it would be considered funny.

"He approached me as I was waiting for a valet to bring my car around. He came up behind me and told me to meet him at the Hayward DMV." She paused anticipating his response of surprise, but Nick was waiting for her to continue.

"Wait a minute, you knew!" She snapped. "You're having me followed too, aren't you?"

Nick looked sheepish.

"Believe me, it wasn't my idea," He said. "Luden's very smart. We didn't want Todd to disappear. We wanted to know what he had to say to you before we snatched him. The DMV came as a complete surprise. We couldn't get close enough."

"He wanted to know if I was wearing a wire," she mused. "Unlike clueless me, he probably already suspected I had a tail."

"It's been suggested. We may have to go with a wire on you."

"No way, I won't have my life open to . . . to gawkers."

"The F.B.I. are professionals, they don't care about your family trees or what you're having for breakfast."

"No wire."

"Okay, let's shelve that for now. What else did Luden have to say?"

Johanna exhaled. "Not much. He wants to meet Leslie. I told him she wants to meet him. He said he would be getting in touch with me soon," she said. "Oh, and I told him Leslie wants me to come with her when they meet—that she trusts me."

Nick threw his pen on the table.

"Are you kidding me?" he said. "Johanna, this is not a game or some hunt for an out of touch ancestor. You could be killed."

"I won't be. I know you're worried, but I know what I'm doing. I'll be careful."

"Will you wear a wire?"

"Nice try, Detective Quinn," she mocked. "No thanks, I'll live longer without one."

CHAPTER TWENTY-TWO

Her mother's townhome, while stylishly decorated, still felt homey and comfortable. Johanna entered using her key and put the bag of pistachio ice cream away in the freezer.

"Johanna," her mother called from upstairs. "Can you check on the casserole in the oven? I'll be right down."

Johanna smiled to herself. Cooking was never her mother's strength, but what she didn't have in producing traditional dishes she made up with delicious and creative embellishments that usually could not be repeated. She peeked in on the casserole.

Maybe manicotti?

"I'm turning it down, Mom," Johanna called up. "It's really bubbling."

Elisabeth Girrard hurried down the steps running her hand through the thick curls of her auburn hair. She moved quickly to give her daughter a kiss on the forehead.

"Thank you, sweetheart, you haven't even taken off your jacket. Just put it on the sofa and pour us both a glass of chardonnay while I rescue our dinner."

Johanna complied.

They spent the next hour chatting over shared memories and the day's happenings. The dish was very tasty, and she had already reached for seconds.

"Mom, what is this dish? It's delicious. I thought I knew what to call it but I'm not sure."

"Ah, hah! I made ratatouille but it looked kind of sad." Her mother grinned. "So, I added ground beef and stuffed it into large manicotti noodles and covered everything in a new spicy sauce recipe."

"Isn't ratatouille a vegetable dish?"

"Are you a vegetarian now?"

"No, but—"

"Exactly, I decided to think out of the box." Elisabeth dabbed her lips with a napkin. "Speaking of decisions, there is something I want to speak to you about."

Johanna paused mid-forkful. "What?"

"I'm getting married."

The food never made it to her mouth. Johanna placed it gently back onto the plate.

"Mom, has Cliff asked you to marry him?"

"No, I asked him, and he said, yes."

Cliff Bennett had been in her mother's life for years. Johanna remembered when he first appeared on the scene when she started college. A former security firm executive, he brought his calm demeanor and seemingly bottomless pit of wisdom to soothe the rancor and instability had resulted from her parents' marriage and eventual divorce nine years earlier. Ironically, she was closer to her parents now that they were no longer together.

Johanna got up and gave her mother a hug.

"I'm so happy for the both of you. When?"

"Soon enough," her mother said. "I want to wait until things are settled at my company. I'm bringing in a new tech unit, and I want to see them firmly engaged. Then, Cliff and I can go down the street to the courthouse, marry, and go on our dream honeymoon to Thailand."

Johanna reached across for her mother's hand.

"Don't elope, I would love to be there."

"Cliff said you would insist," she said. "Alright my darling daughter, when the time comes you will be one of our witnesses."

AVA

AVA GLANCED DOWN AT THE LIST IN HER HAND of numbered boxes. It would be much easier to take the time now to sort through what was going to Australia and what was staying or going into storage. She went to the boxes closest to her office door. Her Legacy clients were all handled except for one retired couple, and Trinidad said she would follow through and prepare the report. She deftly folded flaps of a good sized box and pushed it down the office hall.

"Ava, let me help you," Marty said. "Where are you moving it to?"

"Thank you, slide it inside Trinidad's office."

He lifted the box, placed it in a corner of the office and returned to the lobby desk.

She straightened and rubbed her lower back. "I better get used to bending and shoving. I'll be doing hours of it pretty soon."

"We're going to miss you," he said. "What are you even doing here? Are you all packed? Don't forget the party tonight at Clementine's."

Ava shook her head.

"How can I possibly forget? You guys won't let me," she said. "I wish we could just say goodbye in the office. I'm really not in a jovial mood. There's Eric and . . ." Her voice drifted. "Thank goodness I'm pretty much packed, but I've still got things to do before I leave." She raised her hand before he could speak. "However, I'm resigned to have a good time and make good memories."

"Sorry, do you honestly think there aren't going to be office goodbyes? Well, think again, that's not going to happen. Johanna and Trinidad would be crazy upset, and I would be left behind to listen to their wails—no thanks."

Ava laughed and smiled. "You're right. It's not worth the hassle."

Marty came from around the desk pulling on his hoodie. "Ava, I was going to run out and get a quick sandwich. We're not expecting any clients. Lock the door if you need to leave before I get back, but I shouldn't be long."

"Don't worry, Marty. I've been entrusted with the office before." Ava smiled.

He gave her a mock salute and headed down the corridor.

"Excuse me."

Ava jumped, startled. She turned to the voice belonging to a pale looking young woman standing in the doorway.

"Yes?" she said. "Hello, I'm Ava Lowell, a partner with Legacy Consultants. Our receptionist will be back shortly. Can I help you?"

"I'm not sure. I'm looking for Johanna Hudson. I'm Leslie Todd."

A surprised Ava weaved through a small path of boxes and outreached her hand.

"Leslie, Johanna has told me about you and your grandfather. Does she have an appointment with you today? I think she may be out with another client."

Ava noticed the deflated look on her face.

"No, she didn't know I was coming. She gave me her card and . . . and I guess I thought she . . ."

Ava took Leslie by her elbow and directed her to the conference room gesturing for her to take a seat.

"Can I get you a cup of coffee? Or, water?" Ava asked.

"No, that's okay. Is the office closing?" Leslie nodded toward the boxes.

"What? No, I'm going on a trip. And, I'll be back to the office in a few months. I'm just packing things up," Ava said folding her hands. "Ah, is there anything I can do to assist you?"

Leslie sighed.

"Johanna is helping me meet up with my grandfather. She

found him, or I guess he found her and now he wants to see me, but I've got to tell her when—"

"Todd and Hudson together, this is perfect." One growled.

The voice belonged to one of two men who entered the room swiftly pulling ski-masks over their faces.

Ava was so focused on Leslie's words she didn't notice the invaders until too late. She started to yell but was silenced by a Taser shooting voltage darts into her chest. The excruciating pain caused every muscle and nerve in her body to contract taking her breath away. Mercifully she sank into unconsciousness.

Was that Leslie screaming?

CHAPTER TWENTY-THREE

"**W**HERE'S AVA?" JOHANNA CALLED OUT from her office. "She was here earlier this morning sorting and moving boxes, but she said she had a lot of last minute running around to do," Marty responded. "I slipped out for a sandwich and left her here. When I got back she had already left."

Johanna came out to stand in front of the reception desk.

"She had better not be trying to dodge tonight," she said. "I finalized the catering numbers this morning. And, I was able to get a fantastic DJ. You probably don't know this, but Ava is a wonderful dancer."

"Really?" Marty questioned with more than a little doubt.

"Really." Johanna grinned and then shuffled through a small stack of folders on the counter top. "Did she say anything to you about the papers for the Crossen file? It's the last one she's working on and she said she would leave them on my desk. She must have forgotten."

"That's not the only thing she forgot. She left our door unlocked."

Johanna frowned. "That's not like her at all. She must be more distracted than I thought."

"Good afternoon, everyone," Trinidad entered, wearing a stylish black wool suit and holding a small potted daffodil plant that matched her blouse.

Johanna and Marty exchanged looks of disbelief.

"Good afternoon," Johanna replied nodding to her bundle. "Nice plant, such a . . . a bright yellow. Are you taking up gardening?"

"No, Johanna, I buy because I think it will fill the space on my shelf." Trinidad entered her office continuing to talk. "If I buy a ruler do you think I am taking up house building?"

Johanna looked contrite.

"Good point," Marty mouthed and returned to entering data into the laptop.

Johanna went to the break room and returned with two cups of coffee. She went into Trinidad's office.

"Here, this one is for you." She took a seat. "I thought we could talk a bit about handling the workload after Ava's gone."

"Thank you." She reached for the mug. "I did not mean to rush your feelings."

"Not to worry." She waved the thought away. "Now, financially, were looking pretty good, especially after we get Luden's check."

Johanna accepted the pad of paper and pen that Trinidad slid across the desk.

"Once a week we'll go through our client's status and continue to divide up the cases. I want you to be able to choose the ones which interest you," she said. "Soon, we may have to schedule our intake, too many cases—won't that be great!"

"Yes, and I think it better we take future Luden's payments as an automatic direct deposit."

Johanna agreed.

"Johanna, FedEx just delivered Ava's gift. You want me to put it in the trunk of my car for tonight? Oh, and I've got to pick up our public records order but it won't take me long." Marty offered.

"No, put the Total Station in mine. My car is larger and I padded everything in my trunk so it wouldn't break."

Marty complied. Trinidad came out of her office and watched the lifting of the huge box.

"What exactly is a Total Station?" she asked. "I'm glad Ava will be happy, but I still do not understand it."

Johanna leaned against the wall to let Marty leave. She slid a description page from the cellophane packed instructions taped to the top of the box.

She read, "A Total Station is one of the more valuable items an archaeologist works with. They are extremely useful for getting very precise measurements of where items are both horizontally and vertically. Total Stations are also useful for creating maps of site locations."

Trinidad smiled. "So you do not know either?"

Johanna shook her head. "Not a clue." They both laughed.

"Ava, is always going on about needing one. I knew she would be ecstatic if we gifted it to her. We'll have it shipped once she's settled and has an address." Johanna paused. "Speaking of which have you heard from Ava? I've tried calling and texting her, but she hasn't gotten back."

Trinidad had a thoughtful expression. "No, she has not contacted me. You do not suppose she will not show up tonight?"

"No, Ava wouldn't do that. She knows we're planning a send-off," Johanna said, her mind racing with possibilities.

Trinidad nudged Johanna forward.

"Excuse me," Johanna tapped on the car's passenger window. "I'm Johanna Hudson, I need your help."

It was a reflector sunglass-wearing woman who was following her today. She slid the window down. "Yes, I know who you are Mrs. Hudson, I'm Agent Laura Morris. "How can I help you? Have you seen Carl Luden?"

"No, not yet. But, my partner is missing. Or, at least I can't locate her. It's not like her to not stay in touch."

"Have you seen Ava Lowell since you sit in your car?" Trinidad interjected. "We cannot locate her."

"No, we are focused on Mrs. Hudson. I'll be working surveillance this evening. However, we have an agent inside the building who works the day shift. Let's ask him."

The four of them gathered in Legacy's conference room.

"In three hours, we're having a party to honor my partner. She would not disappear."

Johanna lowered her voice. She was trying hard to keep a grip on her mounting worry. The two agents staring back at her were making Ava's absence seem even more alarming.

"Let's get the CCTV tapes," Morris directed.

They gathered in the building's security center and huddled over a large laptop monitor. It took only a few moments to isolate the lobby during the date and time they sought.

"Oh my goodness," Johanna cried out into her hand and pointed with the other one. "That's Leslie Todd! She was here today? What was she doing here?"

Their client was entering the lobby elevator.

"Too bad we don't have sound. Do you see Luden?" Walters halted the screen.

"No, at least no one I recognize as Luden." Johanna said transfixed.

What was Leslie doing here?

"Let's see where she's going." Morris said.

They switched camera views to the hallway outside Legacy's entrance. There was Marty likely waving goodbye at Ava. Moments later Trinidad and Johanna exchanged looks of dread as Leslie entered Legacy's office. The dread only deepened when minutes later two burly men, visible from the back, strode purposely to Legacy's entry.

Walters stopped the tape.

"Recognize them?"

Johanna and Trinidad transfixed, shook their heads. He started the viewing again.

The tape moved to the view of Ava and Leslie half walking, half dragged to the freight elevator around the corner from the office. Johanna's and Trinidad's faces were transfixed.

"No, no, it cannot be." Trinidad choked out.

Johanna's face, had turned to wet stone.

"Load the outside tape for the rear of the building." Morris said to Walters.

The tape wasn't as clear as the interior version, but it was evident the women were in no condition to walk and had to be carried to a waiting gray van, and shoved inside. The men were now wearing ski masks. They surveyed the empty maintenance lot before climbing inside the vehicle and left. The plates had been muddied over.

There was a long moment of silence in the room.

Walters cleared his throat. "Could one of the men be Luden?"

"No," Johanna said woodenly. "He's not tall or heavy-set."

"Can you think of a reason why they would have wanted to take Ava Lowell?" Morris asked.

"I think they made a mistake. They didn't want Ava—they thought they had me."

JOHANNA REALIZED SHE'D NEVER SEEN NICK in rolled shirtsleeves. He stood in front of the department's video room frowning as he pointed out the various points of possible contact. Paul Kennedy and another agent, who did not introduce himself, sat off to the side behind Johanna and Trinidad. There was a two-way mirror in the rear of the room. In this formal setting she knew Nick would want to keep their relationship quiet—and so did she.

They had been at it for almost two hours. Once Walters and Morris had called in the kidnapping of Leslie and Ava, they had bundled Johanna, Trinidad and Marty into a Mercedes mini-van and took them to a building somewhere in the Livermore Valley having its numerical address as the sole descriptor.

"Detective Quinn, I'm wondering if maybe we need to look at this a little differently." Johanna ran her fingers through her hair. "So far all my meeting interactions with Luden have been at atypical locations. He knows where I am and when I'm going to be there. He's set the logistics."

Kennedy coughed. "We've already had the three of you scanned for tracking electronics—you're clean."

Johanna noticed Trinidad and Marty running their hands over their arms.

"I guess what I'm getting at is Luden may already know his enemies, have taken his granddaughter and my friend." Johanna said. "Either way he will want to get in touch with me. He needs me as his shield to law enforcement."

"What are you suggesting?" Kennedy said.

"Let him," Johanna said. "Let him come to me. You can track him through me."

"You'll agree to a wire?" Quinn asked.

"No, he's already wary," Johanna responded. "But, you can pick out a signal I can give without looking suspect he is making contact. Your people can do a loose surveillance of me, because he'll spot anything close."

"This isn't the movies, Mrs. Hudson," Nick said pointedly. "You are not a professional and we have lives at stake who require more tactics than just willing amateurs."

Johanna winced. "Of course, Detective Quinn, I am more than willing to hear your better proposal."

There was a silence.

"Why don't we take a quick break—ten minutes?" Kennedy said to the room. "We'll return here. Detective Quinn, if you could just hold back a moment."

Kennedy nodded to the quiet figure in the back of the room.

JOHANNA WALKED OUT TO THE PARKING LOT for fresh air, but when she returned to the meeting room Trinidad and Marty were not back, neither was the mysterious guest.

"Owens and Blake are on their way home." Nick answered her unasked question.

"That's right Mrs. Hudson, it's late. But, we're almost finished here. There's just one thing." Kennedy leaned over the table. "We think it best Legacy Consultants go on a hiatus."

"What, you want me to shut the office!" Johanna exclaimed. "I don't see what good that would do. Luden will know you're on to him."

"Maybe, but he'll know for sure you aren't working for the kidnapers. We want him to come to us," Kennedy said.

Johanna rubbed her forehead. She was feeling the weight of the day. She had asked Marty to cancel, to the extent he could, the festivities for Ava's send-off.

"Do what you can, Marty," she said.

Kennedy and Quinn were huddled at the far end of the table. From time they looked up at Johanna. She was emotionally depleted when they finally turned to her.

"Thoughts, Mrs. Hudson?" Quinn asked sympathetically.

"Detective Quinn, wonder if you're wrong. Luden may know where Ava and Leslie could be held. He would slip through by running in the opposite direction to keep from being caught. The bad guys could kill them because it's clear they don't care. The bodies are piling up."

Paul Kennedy slapped his hands on the tabletop.

"I think it's time to call it a night," he said. "Mrs. Hudson an agent is ready to take you home. Get some rest. We'll have a car pick you up at nine a.m. and bring you back here to wrap things up. I'm not going to sugarcoat the situation. We need your help. It's important we find Todd and Lowell as soon as possible. Time is not on their side."

His words sent chills down Johanna's arms.

THE AGENT ASKED JOHANNA TO STEP ASIDE as she went through the house. When she was done she asked Johanna for her phone and entered her number under the emergency tag.

"Don't be afraid to push it, if you feel something is wrong. I'll be on watch outside."

Johanna nodded and locked the door behind her.

She was exhausted and full of worry. The stress of the day had emptied her mental reserves.

Where were they? Were they still alive?

And that's when she saw the voice recorder next to her coffee maker.

CHAPTER TWENTY-FOUR

S HE PICKED UP THE RECORDER AND SAT DOWN at the kitchen
table. Taking a deep breath she pushed the 'Play' button.
It was a poor quality recording:

*Hello, Mrs. Hudson, we will cut to the chase. We thought we
had you, but we are holding Leslie Todd and Ava Lowell. For
now they are safe. Perhaps a little frightened, but that's to be
expected. We want Carl Luden, nothing else. You better hope
he gets in touch with you in the next 24 hours because that's
when we're contacting you with the next step. Follow our
directions and you can take your friends home.*

*We are following you. We know about your visit to the
Feds. If you want to see your friends you won't tell the Feds of
our arrangement. Don't think we won't kill them, because we
will. We've killed before. For us, it's one less trek to the grocery
store.*

*Oh, and by the way this machine was adjusted to play only
one message—once, this one.*

There was a click.
Johanna's hand shook as she hit the 'Playback' button.

Scratchy silence whirred.

Her heart pounding, she went to a drawer and retrieved a quart-sized plastic bag and dropped the device into the sack.

"THANKS FOR GETTING THIS CONTACT TO us first thing this morning," Kennedy said. "It's interesting that his disguise and maneuvers have even stumped his cohorts. Especially if they are relying on you to bring him in."

The group from the night before had reconvened in the sheriff's office in the morning. This time they were in a sterile white room with a white Formica topped table and a large wall screen. After she handed over the recorder, she could tell they were frustrated with the inability of their tech people to retrieve any content.

"We need you to recall every word they said on the tape," Kennedy directed. "It's a vital clue to getting our hands on Luden."

Johanna nodded and repeated the tape message. She only hesitated a moment before telling them the complete missive.

And again, this time they asked her to repeat the communication again into a recording device on the table.

When she finished, an officer came in and left with the machine.

Johanna cleared her throat. "So far this morning, no one here has said anything about rescuing Ava or Leslie. How are you looking out for them?"

"They are our highest priority," said, the yet unidentified agent in the back of the room. He stood and came around the table to the front. He held out his hand.

"My name is Agent Ronald Fuller. I am in charge of seeing your friends are returned safely."

"What are you doing to make that happen?" She asked. "It seems like you are counting on me to pull this off and . . . and I don't know what's going on. My friend . . ." Her voice cracked and she held her head in her hands. She hoped it had the effect she wanted.

Fuller cleared his throat. "Mrs. Hudson, Agent Kennedy and I have been working this case for many months. Your input has been tremendously helpful. It is for your own safety we must limit what we tell you," he paused and continued. "Carl Luden is a desperate man. He has undeclared millions stashed away from his early dealings, money he hid when he went into the protection program, people's pension savings. He only returned part of what he took. We, the IRS, want him, and so do his cronies who did the dirty work while he stole away. The FBI want them and Luden."

"May I see his . . . official, er real photo?" Johanna asked.

She felt her old self this morning, more in control. Not that she had gotten a good night's sleep. She'd laid awake assessing the situation and laying out tactics to extricate Ava and Leslie.

And she had a plan.

"Here it is." Nick slid the shiny image across the table.

Johanna peered at the man in the picture who looked back as if into her eyes. He looked nothing like the man she knew as Carl Luden. Her encounters had been with a jowly, squinty eyed, Santa-faced individual. This man was middle-aged, same squinty eyes, but with a hostile stare and a small keloid scar along the underside of his chin. No wonder they hadn't picked him up.

"And, he looked completely different when he met me at the DMV," Johanna said.

"We know. Compared to the picture you gave our forensic artist yesterday, it's not a surprise we haven't spotted him," Nick echoed her thoughts.

TRINIDAD

TRINIDAD HAD NO WORD FROM JOHANNA. She was probably still meeting with the FBI. She could tell from Johanna's face last night she was hurting very bad. Poor Johanna.

Trinidad had stopped by the office this morning to make the trips to the post office and UPS. They still had clients who were waiting for their charts. She knew Johanna would want to keep up good service.

"We cannot let things drop, Marty."

They shared a cup of coffee in the break room.

"Not to worry. I'll cover the office while you keep appointments. Here's a list for the rest of this week." He handed over a sheet of paper, and then put his hand over hers. "Trinidad, are you okay? This is a lot for me to take in so I can imagine how you must feel."

"I am okay, Marty. What do you say? No worries—yes, I have no worries."

"You may be okay, but you're a lousy liar."

HOUSEWIVES MARKET IN OLD OAKLAND was bustling for a Wednesday morning. The smells of fresh fish, and rows of every cut of meat greeted Trinidad as she walked slowly up and down the aisles of stalls. She didn't expect to be here. She should be watching Ava walk up the ramp at the airport leaving for Australia. Now Ava was gone—maybe forever. No, she would not think it.

She had come here for a quick lunch hoping it would be fairly free of patrons. She was wrong. As she waited patiently in line for her take-out lunch, she was still being jostled.

"Excuse me, Miss," a gravelly voice said in her ear.

She glanced at the cyclist in a blue helmet red sunglasses, and gave him a brief smile of acknowledgement.

He continued, "Perhaps, we could just step outside for a moment."

Trinidad turned to him with a frown. "I am not going to—"

"I'm Carl Luden. Meet me at the plaza in Jack London Square."

She froze. He turned and walked away without waiting for her answer.

It was cool and breezy along the narrow boardwalk. Trinidad sought a concrete bench in the sun near the row of small shops. She was shaking and not just from the cold. Luden had not shown up and she wondered the reasons he could have deliberately sent her on a chase.

Moments later a man appeared with his bike in tow and sat next to her.

"Ms. Owens, thank you for agreeing to meet me."

"I do not remember agreeing."

"And yet you're here."

"Yes, that is true, but maybe not for long," Trinidad said. "Mr. Luden, I must tell you your granddaughter and a dear friend have been taken by your enemies. Johanna, the woman you have been talking to, has been interviewed by the authorities." She spoke straight ahead, glancing at the passersby. "What are you going to do about my friends?"

"I am very familiar with Mrs. Hudson. But this is about what are *you* going to do, Ms. Owens?" He took a cloth out of his back pocket and started wiping the rear bike frame. "If I walk in to the authorities, not only am I a dead man but so is my granddaughter and your friend. And, if I give myself up to . . . to as you say my enemies, who is to say they won't kill Leslie and Ava Lowell anyway? No, I need your help, and you need mine."

"What is it you want me to do?"

"We must find them, and find them soon."

Trinidad exhaled. "Then yes, I will give you my help. What about Johanna?"

"I won't be able to use her as a conduit anymore, too many people on both sides know her as my contact," he said. "So, you're going to have to step-in."

"I do not know what a conduit is, but I will do what it takes to get them home."

"Good. I want you to listen to me, because I don't want anything in writing," he said. "No one can know I am meeting with you. So far you're not being followed. I won't contact you directly unless it is urgent. As for my granddaughter and your friend, there are a few places I know they have used in the past. Let's call them safe houses. It's not likely they would go back to them, but they aren't a bright bunch. I can help I.R.S. by giving them a short list of possibilities of where they might be held."

"If you have this list, Mr. Luden, why do you need me or Johanna?"

He ignored her question. "You can tell them I'll give them the sites, if they will let me go on with my life. Tell Johanna to set up our talk with her boyfriend and the feds. I will get in touch with you with the arrangements."

He stood and righted his bike.

"When?"

"Soon." He got on the bike and spoke over his shoulder. "Tell Johanna."

CHAPTER TWENTY-FIVE

"HE KNEW ABOUT DETECTIVE QUINN, JOHANNA." Trinidad lowered her voice.

They were in the break room and Marty was at the reception desk.

Johanna nodded.

"Well he's right about the fact Leslie that was followed. And, he's right again about you being be the only one who can move around freely without government agents watching your every maneuver."

"He wants me to help him find where they are keeping Leslie Todd and Ava," she said. "He is going to give me a list of places where he thinks they might be."

"Interesting, he expects me to make his deal happen, else why have you tell me about your conversation. I'm thinking he already knows where they are. We are on his game board now." Johanna mused. "Trinidad, you must be very cautious. I don't trust Luden and I don't want you added to the list of 'disappeared.'"

"I will not be disappeared, Johanna. I think it is more likely Mr. Luden will contact me when I am not in the office," Trinidad said. "He will have to do it soon. I do not think the government or the criminals are very patient." She set her shoulders. "I will do the client appointments for you, and the office errands instead of Marty. He will stay here with you."

Trinidad, rinsed her cup in the sink and turned to Johanna with a smile.

"Now I will go to pick up our research materials from the county library before they close. When Mr. Luden contacts me I will send you a text—hmm . . . I'll say . . . 'Remind Marty to change the printer paper.'"

"Then what?"

"Then I will do what he says, and you should too."

"Trinidad, I'm contacting Detective Quinn. If Luden wants to make a deal with law enforcement, good for him. We don't have the resources to run a side investigation. What if we do find the hiding place, what do we do then?"

Trinidad gave a deep sigh. "I do not know. I only want Ava back."

JOHANNA GRASPED HER HANDS AROUND A CUP of weak tepid coffee. The sheriff department's brew machine could use a replacement.

"We got him." Paul Kennedy said, sitting in the interview room in a shirt and tie. "We're going to need to put a tail on Trinidad Owens. The clock is ticking. We snatch Luden as soon as he approaches Owens. His old friends will want him back. And we'll have something to trade for Todd and Lowell."

Nick had been standing by the window, and now he sat down at the head of the table.

"Thanks for coming to us, Mrs. Hudson. I know it must have been tempting to go off on your own." he said. Frowning, he turned to Kennedy. "That plan has a couple of holes. First, we don't know who his old friends are, and now we have no leverage on Luden. We don't have his granddaughter."

Kennedy shook his head. "How about we tell him if he comes on in and cooperates with us, we'll help him see his granddaughter alive and—"

"Gentlemen," Johanna said, holding up her hand and her phone. "Wait, Carl Luden has made contact with Trinidad." She closed her eyes and exhaled. "He's coming in. He wants to see the kidnap video. He has a plan."

TRINIDAD

By THE TIME TRINIDAD TURNED BACK TO THE LOT, he was gone. Out of the corner of her eye, she saw a figure duck behind the parking kiosk in the county library parking lot. She slipped her hand in her jacket pocket and stared a second time at the paper he had given her:

> *I want to see the video.*
>
> *Quinn will bring it, and something to play it on to the Sideboard Community Room at the Castro Valley Library, ten a.m. tomorrow. Johanna Hudson and Trinidad Owens will attend.*
>
> *No other law enforcement or I'm gone for good. I'll just have to see my granddaughter on the other side.*

She had quickly sent the message to Johanna who got the nod from Quinn and Kennedy and called her back immediately.

"Trinidad, come to Detective Quinn's office. They want to see the message." Johanna's voice was rushed and strained. "We're going to find Ava."

CHAPTER TWENTY-SIX

T HE OLD CASTRO VALLEY LIBRARY was no longer owned by the county but was now operated by a community group with an estate annuity from a rich grateful patron. From the outside, it resembled more of a massive craftsman house than the haven it served for the thousands of volumes of books that filled its rooms from floor to ceiling.

"I love the smell of a library," Trinidad whispered to Johanna over her shoulder as they climbed down a wide staircase. "It smells like . . . like—"

"Like all the places you have yet to know?" Kennedy said, behind them.

"Yes," Trinidad looked back and gave him an appraising smile.

"Agent Kennedy, I really don't think you should be here," Johanna interjected. "If Luden sees you, he'll think we're not following his demands, and we will never learn how to find Leslie and Ava."

"Remember, I'm not staying Mrs. Hudson. I'm only here to set the equipment up," he said. "I went over with Detective Quinn how to operate it last night, but it's our equipment and he didn't want to take the chance he couldn't get it up and running. It will only take a few minutes and I'll leave."

I'll bet. Johanna couldn't help thinking.

With one large window looking out onto the beginnings of Chabot Park, the community room was cold from the morning chill outside. As she entered, Nick sent her a nod of acknowledgment. He was already settled in with a coffee machine provided by the library helpers.

The room was good sized with four large metal conference tables placed throughout. The walls held large photographs of the library's historical beginnings. Chairs were stacked along the walls leading to a storage area.

"Morning everyone," Nick said. "Glad to see you're here. Kennedy get this thing going as quickly as you can. I can take it from there."

Kennedy nodded and opened the black case he'd been carrying. Johanna and Trinidad took adjacent seats at the far end of the table. It was clear the seat across from Nick was for Luden.

"Detective Quinn, do you not think this is a strange place for Luden to have a meeting?" Trinidad continued in a whisper, "He can be seen by many people."

The detective snorted. "Not as many as the DMV. I'm sure he's covered his bases."

"You're absolutely right, Detective Quinn, I have." Luden came from the dark corners of the storage room wearing a crossing guard uniform.

"Luden, how did you get in here?" Nick Quinn sputtered. "We had this place checked out."

"I wouldn't brag." Taking the seat, Luden took off his cap. "Johanna, Trinidad, good to see you again. Agent Kennedy we have not met, and while ordinarily I would be furious at the violation of my orders, I appreciate your initiative that you are here due to Detective Quinn's lack of technical skills needed to expedite our task."

He poured himself a cup of coffee. "Let's get this video started."

Minutes later the room was silent as Kennedy clicked off the tape device.

Luden's brow was wrinkled in thought.

Johanna caught the looks between Nick and Agent Kennedy. Still no one said anything until finally Luden exhaled and took a sip of his coffee.

"I think I know where they are," he said. "But, it's not going to be easy. I know these guys."

"Where are they?" Nick urged. "We have support standing by to do what it takes."

"That's what I'm afraid of," Luden mused. "This isn't a sophisticated group. Everything they learned about crime, came from television."

"What do you want for the location information, Luden?" Kennedy prodded.

"To see my granddaughter and forty-eight hours."

"Seeing your granddaughter, that's up to her." Nick shook his head. "About letting you go, sorry you have taken the government for a ride too many times, Luden. We aren't—"

"Detective Quinn, what about Ava?" Trinidad cried out.

Johanna put her hand over her friend's and spoke to Luden, "Now, I know why you wanted us here. You figured we would personalize the pain and the worry. You want our concern for Ava to add to the urgency, and complicate the government's decision."

Luden raised his eyebrow at her comments, but he faced Nick.

"Give me the forty-eight hours and I'll leave you with the list of names of who has control over the cache of money the I.R.S. has been searching for." He turned to Kennedy. "That's the real list you want. It's all you care about right? I told you guys back then and I'm telling you now I turned in all the money I knew about. The rest . . ." He shrugged. "These are the guys you want."

"You're lying. They are looking for you because they know you have their money." Quinn smirked. "The list you're talking about, if you were truthful, would only have one name on it—yours. You want us to shield you from them. Why are they willing to face federal kidnap charges? Because they must think you have access to their money."

"People," Johanna exclaimed. "We are wasting time speculating,"

Nick nodded in agreement and pointed at Luden. "How's this sound? You retrieve the government's money from whatever hole you've hidden it and identify where the hostages are being held. When you hand off the cash to your cohorts, and get the hostages released, we'll be there to make the arrests. But, just in case you change your mind, again, when we locate Leslie Todd and Ava Lowell we will detain your granddaughter until we have the money and the crooks. If you renege, we will arrest your granddaughter for conspiracy in the murders of Philip Nava and Eric Lowell."

"And me?" Luden asked.

Kennedy gave him a cold stare. "We know we can't arrest you for the past, but after this the government is through with you." He leaned over the table. "Don't spit on the sidewalk."

Johanna and Trinidad exchanged looks of hope.

"It's not as straightforward as you think." A solemn-face Luden rubbed his forehead. "The thing is their leader is skittish and doesn't always think before he acts. He's probably very nervous right now. He'll reach out to me soon, but it would be better if I get to him first."

"No more talking." Kennedy stood gathering his files. "Let's get the show on the road."

Nick picked up his folder and headed for the door.

"Just a moment." Luden coughed. "There's a matter of the money. I don't have it on me. I have to retrieve it. It's not far. I'll need to go in first. If they see you, they could kill your friends and vanish. So, I'll go in, give them the money and come out with the hostages."

"We're not letting you or the money out of our sight." Nick barked returning to his seat with a hard stare. "Don't test us Luden, you'll come up the loser."

Luden held up his hands.

"I'm going to have to give them their portion. I promised them they would share in it. That's why they're looking for me, so they know there's no trap. You can chase them down after the take-down—you'll have the list, remember?""

"Are you crazy, we're not letting you walk away with thirteen million dollars?" Kennedy said. "We're keeping an eye on you. If we had our choice you'd be in prison."

Johanna noticed a flicker of something flash across Luden's eyes. Was there more than thirteen million at play?

"Just to be clear," Johanna said, putting her hand out to speak. "Let me see if I understand the plan," her voice rose. "Luden gets the money from wherever he's hid it. I go with him to the hiding place. The feds let him take the money to the bad guys to res-cue Ava and Leslie. The feds will track us from a distance, mak-ing sure the ransom money is paid and the hostages retrieved. Then, with an all clear signal the police will close in, arrest the criminals, take back the money, and as a bonus they let Luden get away. Do I have it right?"

Luden smiled. "It's a win-win."

Out of the corner of her eye Johanna caught Kennedy's swift movement as if to land a punch. He was stopped by Nick's left shoulder.

"Nice try, Luden," Nick said. "There is no way we're going to let you out of our sight with the money. Tell us where you're hiding it. Or, else there's a jail cell three floors below us with your name engraved on the door."

"Detective Quinn, what about Ava?" Johanna's question was more of a plea. She turned to Luden. "That's why I need to go with him. I can be the guarantee to make sure he follows through."

"No, way." Nick Quinn protested. "That's not a guarantee we can approve."

"Hmm, but it's not a bad idea," Luden said contemplatively. "We can leave this evening."

"Mrs. Hudson, do you know what you're saying?" Kennedy said. "Now, he'll have three hostages."

Johanna shook her head. "I know what I'm suggesting detectives and yes, I'm scared. But I also know Ava Lowell saved my life when I was in a very dark emotional place, I wouldn't be here but for her. Now, it's my turn—you make this transfer happen."

Nick and she exchanged a long look.

Nick Quinn reached for Luden's collar forcing him to straighten in his seat. "If anything happens to Johanna or the other hostages, I will personally make sure you never take another breath of freedom."

"No need to get ugly, Detective. I'll make it easy for you," Luden said not smiling as he smoothed his shirt. "What Johanna proposes could work nicely. I'll take her with me. Oh, and no tags. I'll know, and the deal is off. If anyone gets killed, you'll be responsible." He paused. "I'll retrieve the money from its current placement and she'll hold on to it until we get to the location. I'll have to let them know I'm coming. Johanna will then contact you. She'll verify her friends are safe and released. She's your insurance. You'll arrest the bad guys, get your money and then give me enough time to get away."

"Too complicated, and too dangerous," Kennedy barked. "You tell us where the money is! Where are Lowell and Todd being held?" He slammed his fist on the table.

Johanna winced.

Luden just smiled. "We're wasting time gentlemen."

CHAPTER TWENTY-SEVEN

IT WAS LATE. IT HAD BEEN A LONG DAY, and it wasn't nearly over. Johanna had come into the office to wait for Luden to contact her. The plan was for him to get the money, pick her up they would drive together to the hostage site. She sat staring out the window onto the small park next door.

For the first time in a long time Johanna was overcome with anxiety and worry. It must have shown in her face. Trinidad and Marty were failing at trying to find things to do to fill the time of waiting.

"This is not a good idea," Trinidad pleaded. "Let me hide in the trunk. We do not know if Carl Luden's friends are still guarding them. We do not even know if . . . if they are still alive."

Johanna sat on her shaking hands. "Please, don't worry, Trinidad. You and Marty go home. You need to be here tomorrow. Monday is our busiest day."

Marty gave her a hug. "I'll keep everything together."

"Good, the office will be taken care of," Trinidad said. "I think you will need me. Promise me, Johanna, to be unbelievably careful. I do not trust Mr. Luden."

Johanna shoved them out the door. "Go."

Evidently the lack of trust was mutual. Luden had secured a rental car. He appeared quietly in Legacy's lobby area. He had taken the back stairs and pointed to them now.

"Just in case, they're thinking of tracking us," he said watching Johanna shoulder her purse. "We'll take these. Oh, and I'll take your cellphone, please."

"How will I contact Detective Quinn?"

"You can use my phone when we get there. He'll be able to track you. I won't be using it where I'm going after this, anyway."

She handed over the phone with a sigh of resignation. He placed it in her desk drawer and nodded toward the door. "Now, let's go."

Luden kept his eyes on road. They drove in silence.

The Tule fog had already started to seep into Napa's expansive valley. Like a thick blanket of cloud it hovered over the ground resulting in cushioned sound. From the rambling incline of the Silverado Trail, Johanna could hardly tell if it was dawn or dusk. But, soon it would be nightfall and the weaving roadway was already reflecting the headlights from a few periodic cars.

They were going back to the tunnel house.

It didn't take her long to realize their destination. It made sense, they were headed for the lair he had made for himself. And when she thought about it, with its warren of aging underground tunnels and dead-end caves it was a perfect place to hold hostages. Since the late 1870's winery tunnels and caves were constructed as a natural insulator with high humidity and constant temperature to nurture the cherished grapes of the valley's renowned wines. Some houses had over 35,000 square feet of caves. It had be for these reasons and the fact Luden was counting on the police never thinking the house would once more be used for crime.

"I remember this way. This is where Phillip Nava was killed," Johanna broke the silence. "Do you know if Ava is okay? Are you in contact with your . . . your men?"

"They just want the money—not trouble. They'll be guarding them until we show up with it and they get their share."

She noticed Luden didn't really answer her question.

"And, after?" She prodded.

"After that," he paused. "After that, we will all be on our way."

"How soon will I see Ava and Leslie?" She pressed. "When will I be able to contact Detective Quinn?"

"Like I said, when I'm on my way." Luden stared straight ahead. "I'm sure you can understand my caution." He turned to look at her. "Don't worry Johanna. You have been fair to me. I will deliver you and your friends safely."

Don't worry.

LOW LIGHTS FLICKERED FROM THE SMALL HOUSE as it appeared at the base of the hill. In the fog it had a chilling effect and Johanna drew herself up realizing despite Carl Luden's reassurance, these might be her last minutes on earth.

There was a car parked on the gravel path leading to the forlorn structure. He pulled in next to it.

The front door opened before they opened their car doors, and a man appeared.

"That you Carl?" He called out in a muffled voice. "You got the money? We kept them just like you said."

Johanna couldn't believe her ears. He had manipulated them all. She wasn't surprised, only amazed at his brazenness.

"You lied!"

Luden shrugged.

The captor wore a mask and a white hazmat suit, much like the getup they had when they took Ava and Leslie a few days ago. Johanna forced herself to take a deep breath. She knew it was a good sign they wanted to make sure they couldn't be identified by the survivors.

It meant they were planning for survivors.

"Yeah, it's me." He motioned with his head toward Johanna. "Remember, no names." He walked past Johanna. "I got the money."

Johanna, momentarily frozen in place, stared at his back as he walked into the house carrying what appeared to be a backpack. She hurried behind him.

Her voice faltered. "Are they safe?" She made her way behind Luden into the front room. Johanna took a breath of faked confidence. "We want to see them before you take off with the money."

"Lady, are you kidding me. You got no leverage in this game." The man said shutting the front door behind her, and faced Luden.

"Get the team together in the back," Luden said. "We'll distribute shares and you guys can be on your way."

Johanna whipped around to face Luden and slowly shook her head.

"You! You're one of them! I . . . I believed you . . . wha . . ." her words stumbled to a disbelieving stop. She took a breath and spat out. "Where is Ava? Was Leslie in on this too?"

Luden reached into the drawer of the sole piece of furniture in the room and pulled out a ring of keys.

"Speaking of which, do you want to see your friends or not?"

Johanna's frown was accompanied by a set jaw outlining her anger and frustration. Her mind quickly assessed her new circumstances.

"Where's Ava?" She said. "I take it your granddaughter is well. You don't seem to be concerned about her."

"Mrs. Lowell is fine." Luden said smoothly, not responding to her last comment. "My team here have assured me she has been well-treated. You will see her soon enough."

His "team" member coughed into his fist and motioned for Luden toward the rear of the cabin. Luden gave him a brief nod, and shifted the backpack of money onto his back. He turned to Johanna.

"Johanna, there's not a lot of time left for this to play out. I have no doubt your detective has scrambled his tech gurus to respond from information supplied by the charming Trinidad Owens. He assuredly has the government hounds trying to track our steps."

Luden gave her a look of reprimand. "Unfortunately, he will be unsuccessful."

"Cut the lecture, Luden. If there's little time, where is Ava?" Johanna said through gritted teeth.

He tilted his head at her and began rummaging through a second backpack he pulled from a cabinet.

He gestured to his partner. "Escort my granddaughter into the kitchen." He took a small pistol from the inside of his pant leg next to his ankle. He motioned it toward Johanna to move back. "And, get ready to bring Mrs. Lowell into the front room when I tell you."

Johanna took a step back, confused by the mixed signals Luden was giving off.

The man edged forward and cleared his throat. Johanna could tell he was still trying to gesture something was wrong. So could Luden. He moved away and they whispered just of reach of Johanna's hearing. The man left.

Luden spoke hurriedly, "Mrs. Hudson, Johanna, I am under no illusion that I can trust you so I'm afraid I'm going to have to place you in zip ties while I get an assessment of current conditions." He nudged her to turn around. "Remember, the longer you take to comply, the less time I have to get away, forcing me to be less accommodating to my . . . guests."

"You don't trust me? Guests! You mean hostages!" Johanna spat out. "I—"

"You see Johanna, this is what I'm talking about—you're taking up precious time. I must see to my team's departure. The masks work both ways. No can identify anyone else. This is not my real face. I planned it that way. They have already started to evacuate. There are only a few left now." He reached for a half-opened box on the mantle and pulled out a set of ties. "Soon, I will take you and Mrs. Lowell down to a labyrinth of tunnels that wind their way under this house. Your detective friend will have to choose which one we took and which one leads to you. Unfortunately, if he guesses wrong there may be an issue of available oxygen."

"What about Leslie . . . and the money . . . and turning in your team to the feds?"

"I don't think I said *I* would be turning the team in. I said the feds could apprehend them with the money." Luden gave her a half grin, "*My* money is in a safe place—with me. I earned it. And my granddaughter, well she's coming with me. Blood is thicker than water, and law enforcement should focus on the real bad guys."

"That money isn't yours. But don't worry I'm not going to try and convince you. You *are* the bad guy." Johanna said, her eyes frantically searching the room for invisible help. "Why did you have to drag us into your scheme? We never did anything except try to support Leslie."

"It is because you showed such kindness to my granddaughter that I am offering you escape."

Escape?

"Why did you involve me in all of this drama anyway?" Johanna prodded. "I supplied you with an alibi for Nava's killing. You were back in your granddaughter's good graces. The Feds were all over me—not you, and what about your friends—they were breathing down my neck not yours. Why are you bothering with me?"

"As it turned out, I didn't have to." Luden shrugged, but didn't drop his arm that held the gun. "But, I felt . . . sorry for what happened to your husband and child. That was a dirty deal."

Johanna stiffened, her throat tightening.

"I even thought about giving you a share of the money." He straightened when she started to protest. "No, no don't worry. I know you might think of it as blood money, but it's all I have to offer to show my regret."

"Your regret!" Johanna yelled. "Are you kidding me? You're telling me you killed off my family and now you've kidnapped my best friend. Can you hear yourself? You're a monster."

His face flushed. "I won't take that personal. Your being . . . upset is understandable."

"Take it personal." She mentally scrambled to stall. "How will you get away if you kill me? You'll be a wanted man—more wanted than you are now."

He mused. "You're right, I guess that won't work out."

Johanna peered at him closely. His words sounded almost unhinged.

"Where's Leslie?" she asked softly.

Luden did a rapid blink of the eyes, paused then said, "She will have a normal life without her criminal family and lowlife boyfriend to burden her. Her mother had a trust that will go to her—that's the only way the feds will let her keep the money. It wasn't the result of a crime. She won't get all I wanted her to have, but she'll have enough."

"But she won't have her grandfather, her only living relative. She'll—"

He frowned. "Leslie is family. She'll have to make a choice." He lowered the gun then raised it again. "The fact she was even interested in locating me, means family is everything."

"You set me up to find Nava."

"True." Luden shrugged. "But, I did the world a favor." He peered at her.

"What! Leslie said she picked Legacy because of the newspaper coverage. Did she know Nava was here?" Johanna voice chilled. She tried to focus on calming her rapid heartbeat. She took a deep breath and said in disbelief. "You had your granddaughter's fiancé killed."

"Best wedding gift I could give her." He snorted.

He approached her.

"Wait," she said. "Wait."

"Behind your back, your hands . . . now."

Johanna did as he said.

He pulled tight on the ties. Then, she felt a sharp prick in her arm, and as if in slow motion, she slid to the floor.

JOHANNA BLINKED HER EYES AND SHOOK HER HEAD. The blurriness was slow to go away. It didn't help the room was dark except for a dim light emanating from a metal sconce on a far wall. It must be battery-powered. She was on a bed—no a cot. She tried to lift herself up, but her head started spinning. Then there was the smell of mold. She dropped back.

A sound came from across the room. A moan. She was not alone.

"Who's there," her voice cracked.

There was no answer, only another moan.

She bit down on her lip. The pain helped to clear the fog in her head. Once more she raised herself on her elbows and squinted into the shadows. A figure was huddled in a fetal position on another cot.

"Hello," she said in a loud whisper. "Ava, is that you?"

No answer.

Johanna brought herself to a sitting position. Her eyes were adjusting to the gloom. The figure wasn't Ava. It was much too long, too big. A man. She steadied herself to stand bracing against a wall with her outreached arm. A shot of pain flashed through her head. She took a halting step toward the cot, then stopped.

Ropes.

Snakelike they wrapped around his feet. She couldn't see his hands.

Where was she? Her memory still felt like a wad of cotton, but she remembered Luden and she remembered vaguely being carried—but nothing else.

Why was this man tied up? Friend or foe? Moving closer she could tell it was indeed a man. His back was to her, his arms holding knees to his chest.

"Hello, are you all right?"

She leaned over to touch his shoulder. Nothing. But she had a feeling he knew she was there. He stiffened.

"My name is Johanna Hudson. I'm looking for my friend Ava Lowell." She paused.

He straightened his legs and fumbled to right himself.

Finally, his body made the turn to face her. Johanna's eyes grew wide and she put her hand over her mouth.

"Jo?"

Eric!

EVEN IN THE HAZY LIGHT SHE COULD MAKE OUT her now gaunt friend. He wore the start of a beard and fronted a scraggly mat of hair. She bent over him lifting aside the thick rope that allowed 2 feet of gap between his hands. His legs were chained in the same way as his hands. A whiff of confinement odor caused her nostril to wrinkle.

"Eric, how . . . I mean what . . ." she stumbled over her words.

He fell back onto the bed seemingly spent. "It's a long story," he said in a cracked voice. He pulled free a plastic bottle of water squeezed between the wall and the bed and once more partially sat up to take a deep swallow. "Jo, it's been a nightmare and I would like to take the time to explain everything to you—but you don't have much time." He coughed several times. "When they come back, you must—"

He coughed repeatedly.

"I'm ready." Johanna reassured him, wincing at the lingering ache in her head, but wanting to give him a hug. "What can I do? I'm not sure the police know where we are and—"

The door creaked open.

CHAPTER TWENTY-EIGHT

J OHANNA STARTLED, LOOKED UP AND STARED at Luden who entered the room with a grim look and with another disguise.

"Where are Ava and Leslie?" she said blinking repeatedly to try and keep her head clear. She ignored her rapid heartbeat and the feel of cloth that seemed to fill her mouth.

"They're close by." Luden he replied looking around her at the figure on the bed. "Aren't you surprised to see your old friend, Eric Lowell? This will be a regular reunion."

He went over and patted Eric on his head. A plaintive moan escaped Eric's lips.

"Stop it." Johanna called out, stumbling to her friend's side. "What's the matter, Eric? What's wrong with your head?"

"I'll be okay." Eric gave her a lopsided woeful look. "It's my eye, Jo. They had to make sure I wouldn't escape, that I wouldn't go back to the police. Where they hit me I don't see well, and my leg's messed up. They were going to use me to ramp up the stakes. They told me everyone would think I was tied in with their group."

"Oh, Eric. We didn't know, Ava didn't know. She was—"

"Okay, okay," Luden said. "Enough with the get together. Let's talk about what's going to happen next. If you want to see your friend, you will do exactly as I say."

He positioned himself in front of the door.

"First, to show you I'm not a monster, there is a wheelchair waiting outside this door at the entrance to the tunnel passages. Johanna, you will push Eric Lowell in the chair, and take the tunnel to your freedom. As I said, I will set you on your way. Then I will start my leave time, along with my granddaughter, and we will strike out on our own."

"Leslie is going with you?" Johanna frowned. "What's the catch? This sounds too . . . too considerate. What about Ava?"

"Ava?" Eric said. "I don't understand. What about Ava?"

"No time now, Johanna, will explain everything to you, later," Luden replied. "We will make our way to Mrs. Lowell's . . . er, room and she will join you on the way out." Luden looked at his watch. "Enough explanations, I don't think you understand what you will be facing if we don't get moving. Either you do as I say—now, or a member of my very greedy and heartless team will kill you. To them you're hostages and unfinished business. I told them I wouldn't give them their money, until they were ready to retreat and you were on your way. I am giving you a chance."

"I don't—"

"Johanna, you have thirty seconds to move out into the corridor where there will be a man and a chair waiting. If you take one second longer—you're on your own." Luden crossed his arms.

"Do it, Jo." Eric called out in a hoarse voice. "At least we have some kind of chance."

Johanna exhaled. "All right, yes. Let's go."

THE CORRIDOR WAS DARK. JOHANNA REALIZED immediately the room that had held them had been in a narrow cave. It was crudely constructed with a dirt floor and rough rocks lining the walls in a haphazard pattern. The vague scent of kegged wine lingered as they entered the passage.

She frowned as Eric slumped over when Luden's man untied

him. With minimal care Eric was placed in the wheelchair and strapped in. She winced as he groaned.

"For the pain," Luden smiled, as he revealed a hypodermic needle and gave him an injection.

Johanna protested, "He's already out of it."

"The medication is already making him drowsy, he's fine." Luden remarked.

Fine, really?

Luden gave his team member the nod to leave.

"I'll lead the way," Luden directed Johanna. "If you will please push Lowell."

They started the trek down a darkened path.

"Where's Ava?" She asked, looking down on her sleeping passenger.

"Don't worry, your friend is just ahead." Luden turned a corner and pointed to a light under a door down a narrow passage. "See, I kept my word. Here's the key."

Johnna parked the chair and took the key. She made her way to the door. It was heavy oak. She put the key in the lock, turned and pushed.

The room was small and looked to have served as a storage area for what appeared to be wine-making supplies. The low battery light emanated from a small lamp set between two twin beds. One bed was empty and sitting on the other bed, Ava stared at her.

"Ava!" She rushed to her friend's side.

Johanna was met with a blank stare and a lack of recognition.

Ava had always prided herself on her appearance, even at a dig site as she shoveled dirt looking for finds. She always looked put together. Johanna remembered her camp photos. But not now, her clothes were rumpled and soiled. Her face had streaks of dirt.

Johanna took a deep sigh, swiped at her tears as she squeezed hard the shoulders of her friend in a long-delayed hug.

Ava's eyes stared back at her, but her Ava was gone.

And when she turned around, so was Luden.

Johanna peered out into the darkened passage and fought down the panic creeping up her chest. She exhaled and turned back to Ava who had not moved from the bed where she sat.

"Ava," she said gently. "It's Johanna, can you hear me? Can you stand . . . walk?"

She wanted to cry when Ava, looking past her and zombie-like, stood.

"Yes! Okay, this is progress," Johanna spoke quickly and rubbed her friend's arms and hands. "Ava, we have to find a way out of here. We may not have a lot of oxygen. But, we can do this. And . . ."

Johanna paused when her friend looked at her, really looked at her, with her friend's own tears flowing. Ava put her hands down and looked up with a wrinkled brow.

"Johanna?"

"Yes, my dear Ava, it's me. Welcome back."

"Where . . . how? They kept me here." Ava voice came back as if from a trance. "They . . . they took Leslie away, and then I think they must have drugged me. How long have I been here?"

"Almost two days." Johanna said, looking around the room for anything they could use to light their journey. "Ava, you won't believe who I have with me. He's in the corridor."

"He?"

"It's Eric, he's alive."

Her friend slid down to the floor in a faint. Johanna lightly slapped her face.

"Ava, sorry I didn't mean to shock you. But, we've got to go. Luden has left us to find our own way out."

Ava took a couple of deep breaths and stumbled into the passage-way. When she saw Eric, she bent over and hugged her ex-husband. He was still groggy from the sedation and didn't respond. Shaking with more tears, she cradled his head in her arms. Ava looked over to catch Johanna's eyes. They exchanged knowing looks.

Ava took another deep breath, and after a shaky attempt to straighten her back said, "Okay, let's get this show on the road."

"I think we should go back the way we came," Johanna said. "We went past two other passages, and I think there was a dim light down the one where Luden walked me."

"I'll push Eric, you take the lead." Ava nodded and pointed the chair in the direction Johanna pointed. "And, as my fellow dig partners would say, *when you don't know where you're going, any road will take you there.*"

"Do they really say that?"

"No, I was being optimistic, what they really say is, *what doesn't kill you makes you stronger.*"

TRINIDAD

TRINIDAD NEVER GOT HEADACHES, but she had one now.

She had tucked herself in a chair in the corner of the sheriff's conference room hoping not be noticed. She told them she found Johanna's phone in her desk, they wouldn't be able to track it. Detective Quinn had a car pick her up and bring her and the phone to the department. It was during the quick ride she remembered Johanna's tale of discovering Phillip Nava's body and the house of tunnels.

At the police department, Trinidad shared her belief that Johanna and Luden were headed for the Napa location. Evidently, Agent Kennedy and Detective Quinn had the same idea, but wanted more than a strong guess. They were waiting for Johanna to make contact, but there had been no word. That was almost an hour ago and it was getting late. Now they were talking about rushing the house.

She cleared her throat. "I want to go too," she said.

Heads turned to her.

"Not a good idea," Nick Quinn smiled. "We appreciate everything you've done to help. But if we're going to save your friends, this is for trained professionals only. In fact, we heading out in five minutes."

"I know how to get in touch with Luden," she blurted.

They stopped in the doorway. Detective Quinn turned around with a frown matching the one on Agent Kennedy's face.

"Miss Owens, we are wasting time," Quinn said. "What are you saying?"

Kennedy rubbed his hands over his head. "How can you contact him?"

"I have his phone number." Trinidad moistened her lips. "He'll answer when he sees my number."

Detective Quinn shook his head. "Let me guess, you'll give us his number if we let you come along."

"Yes, and like you said, we do not have enough time." Trinidad stood, slinging her purse over her shoulder. "I know you think you can probably trace his calls, but you do not have my phone number, and precious time will have passed for the warrant you will need to take it from me."

The two men exchanged looks.

Quinn scowled. "All right, you can come with us, but you will not be able to leave the car." He held out his hand. "We'll take the phone now."

Trinidad pulled back.

"No, detective, I will hold onto the phone until we get there." She smiled. "I have to be with my friends. I know you are concerned about involving people who are not police, but I promise to stay out of the way of harm."

Detective Quinn gave her a long look. "Then let's get going."

SHE WASN'T RELIGIOUS, BUT TRINIDAD PRAYED NOW.

Sitting in the back seat, as Agent Kennedy sped the car down the highway, she could not ignore the feeling of unease encompassed her. Too much time was passing, too much time for Carl Luden to get away, and too much time for Johanna and Ava to be on their own facing danger.

She chewed her bottom lip.

Too much time was slipping away.

"We're just a few minutes from the house," Quinn said over his shoulder as if reading her thoughts. "We are going to need you to call Luden now. That was the deal. We need to get a location on him."

"Of course," Trinidad said. "Yes, it the deal. But what about Johanna and Ava? How do we know they are okay? Maybe if we waited to call him when we get there, we could see if—"

"No, Miss Owens," Kennedy said looking into the rear view mirror. "We don't have any more time. We have to get our people in place. Call him now."

Trinidad nodded. She hoped her brag about Luden's response to seeing her name would work out in the real world. She had gambled. She punched the number.

"Miss Owens," Luden responded after one ring. "I'm not surprised to hear from you. In fact, I was expecting it. You discovered the location. I take it you are calling about your friends. Please forgive me, but I don't have time for details. I only took your call to tell you everyone is fine, for now. Tell Detective Quinn and Agent Kennedy not to waste time tracking my phone—I installed a cell signal block in the tunnels. Goodbye."

"But—"

The connection was gone.

Kennedy and Quinn exchanged looks. They drove the rest of the way in silence.

"That's it up ahead." Quinn said nodding toward the small house with a single window in front.

Agent Kennedy talked into his phone—he was calling in to request support, "Get the drones out here. We should be able to get some kind of thermal imaging signal."

Detective Quinn sounded skeptical after the call ended. "These passages are pretty deep. There's a chance we won't be able to pick up body heat."

"Maybe," Trinidad spoke up from the back seat. "But wonder if it does."

Darkness was starting to fall, and Trinidad took in the forlorn-ness of the site. There was one car visible in the dimness of the scene. They pulled up behind it.

Kennedy and Quinn got out and huddled briefly.

Quinn came back to her and opened her door. "Stay here, Miss Owens. Under no circumstance are you to get out of this vehicle. We kept our promise, now you keep yours. We called in some special troops to find Jo . . . Mrs. Hudson and Mrs. Lowell, and they will. Let them do their job by staying out of the way. If we have to rescue you, that's less time we can give them."

She nodded. "I understand, Detective."

As she spoke, cars were pulling up behind them with uniformed men and women jumping out and running into the house.

He waved them on, then peered at her. "You stay here and try not to worry. We'll get them back." He gave her a last stern look, turned and followed the others into the house.

"You can trust us."

Trinidad waited until the front yard was cleared of law enforcement, except for the two officers talking as they guarded the front door. Ducking in the shadows, she slipped out the other side car door and headed to the far edge of the house.

CHAPTER TWENTY-NINE

"IT IS THOUGHT THE ANCIENT EGYPTIANS had a plan to not get lost when digging tunnels," Ava said, getting in place with Eric behind Johanna. "Place your hand, whichever one is nearest a wall, onto the wall, and follow it. It doesn't matter which wall, but don't change hands. Then keep walking, maintaining contact between your hand and the wall. Eventually, we'll get out."

Johanna frowned. "Sounds too simple. Are you sure?"

"Trust me, I make my living digging up trails and tunnels," Ava replied testily. Then she looked around her. "We need to get going."

"Luden said there might be an issue with oxygen." Johanna started walking steadily along the path ahead of her.

"I'm afraid he's right," Ava said pushing a half-conscious Eric over the uneven floor. "Underground space has unique environmental characteristics due to its particular geographical location; a typical characteristic is the enclosed environment below the surface of earth, which is prone to cause decreased oxygen concentrations and increased carbon dioxide concentrations, elevated humidity and—

"Enough, I get it," Johanna shook her head. "No breathable air."

They walked in silence for many minutes until the light from the battery lantern flickered in Johanna's hand.

"Great, no air and maybe no light."

"Just don't take your hand from that wall," Ava warned.

What Johanna didn't mention was they had been walking far longer than the path she and Luden had taken. Then there was that faint odor of mold that persisted. Also, the path was bumpier and more pitted than she recollected. Eric's chair was taking major dips and bumps.

"Where am I?" His voice cracked.

"Eric, it's Ava." She bent down and touched his face. "We're in a tunnel maze. I can't believe you're alive. I've been . . . I've been so worried."

"Ava? It's you? Ava, Ava," he exclaimed. "Please, we have to talk." He visibly strained to see in the darkness. "Listen to me, where's Carl Luden? We have got to get away. My head, my eye is . . ." He continued to squint. "Do you have any water?"

Johanna handed him the bottle they had retrieved from his cot. He swallowed deeply then stopped.

"We're going to need to share this, I've had enough." He handed the bottle back to Johanna. "What's our situation?"

"Our situation is we're doing our best to get out of here before our oxygen runs out." Johanna replied. "I smell mold too, that can't be good."

"Wait," Ava chuckled. "That's not mold, that's *Mi Fleur*. It's Leslie Todd's fragrance. It's a good sign: it means she's been in these corridors. Maybe we're close."

"Interesting, I didn't know you were a fashionista." Johanna smiled.

"I'm not, but I had to do a lot of shopping prepping for the dig, and it was being promoted in all the department stores."

"Luden said Leslie would be going with him. I don't think we can count on her."

"No, it doesn't sound like it." Ava agreed. "It's too bad, but I guess family won out—what a family."

They shifted Eric so he could sit as comfortably as possible, and they once more started down the path. Johanna continued to press her hand against the wall.

What time was it?

She was so tired, the drugs she'd been given were still clouding her brain and slowed her down. However, she knew Nick and Agent Kennedy were out there, somewhere, trying to find them. She was counting on Trinidad to remember their conversation about Luden's hideout. Hopefully she'd make the connection of his possible return to the scene of the crime.

They walked on.

Ava's silence spoke her worry. Eric murmured and was weaving in and out of coherence. Johanna kept putting one foot in front of the other, until she came to a dead end. She blinked back tears and caught Ava's eyes in the dim light.

"Okay, so we go back a few yards and follow the path to the right," Ava said already turning Eric's chair around. "Believe it or not, this is a good sign. Now, place your hand alongside the other wall."

Johanna looked at her friend wondering if this was more false hope than archeological certainty. Still, she nodded and took a deep breath reaching for the wall across and took steps in the new direction.

"We are getting out of here," she said. "Do you hear me, Ava? We are getting out of here. I—"

She stopped speaking. There was a faint noise, a scrape maybe. Johanna held up her hand and held her breath.

Nothing.

Ava gave her a rueful smile and they started down the new passage and more tunnel. Minutes passed, and the sound came again. This time Johanna could tell Ava had heard it too.

"Hello, can you hear me? We're here." Johanna yelled. "Help!"

But there was nothing.

Ava placed her hand on Johanna's arm. "Better conserve our oxygen. I hate to suggest it, but we'll do better using the chair to make sounds. The metal will reverberate." She looked down on

Eric. "I'm so sorry." She pushed his chair, scraping the stone with a screeching noise that echoed loudly in the darkness. He moaned but said nothing.

Johanna saw his face had turned deathly pale hosting a growing swollen purple and red mass that covered his eye. His head rolled, she could tell the chair colliding with the wall had caused punishing pain.

They walked on holding to a steady but slowing pace. Then Johanna paused and exhaled. If she could just sit down. If she could just . . .

She sniffed.

"Ava, do you smell it? Do you smell *Mi Fleur*?"

Her friend smiled. "Yes, I do. It's pretty strong too." She wiped her forehead. "Remember, don't take your hand from the wall. This may be the pathway." She bent down over Eric's head. "I'm so sorry to do this, but we have to get their attention." She once more thrust the chair's wheels against the wall.

Johanna grimaced at the sound.

Eric screamed and passed out.

TRINIDAD

THE SLOPE WAS MUDDY AND TRINIDAD kept slipping as she made her way around the side of the house, but she was determined. Using her phone flashlight found herself at a *ducto de ventilacion*. Just like the hollows at home.

She could hear orders being shouted inside the house. They were going down into the caves. What did Johanna always say: ask for forgiveness and permission? Or, was it not forgiveness and later permission? Whatever.

She dug inside her purse for the roll of twisted twine. The police might have the sophisticated technology, but in her country of Trinidad the twine had saved many a lost child. The major difference was at home the victims weren't deliberately left to die. She tied the twine in multiple knots to an adjacent grate and put the extra roll of twine and her phone in her jacket pockets. She left her purse behind.

Trinidad half crawled—half slid down the narrow metal vent. She wasn't claustrophobic, but the constricted area made her glad she had on her simple workout clothes. She crawled forward for many minutes turning down vent tunnel after vent tunnel, always taking the one on the right, gripping the twine as it unwound. Then she heard it.

A far away scraping noise.

She called out, "help is coming."

There was no response.

CHAPTER THIRTY

"**L**EAVE ME HERE," ERIC SAID, turning his shoulder to face Ava. "You two can make faster progress without me."

"No, that's not going to happen. I'll stay here with you." Ava brushed her sleeve across her moist forehead. "Johanna, you go ahead and bring back our rescue."

Johanna shook her head. "Both of you forget about it; we stay together. That's what they always tell you in disaster training."

She gave Ava a look assuring her there was no use arguing. They trekked on.

The tunnel had started to curve but it was also dipping downward. Ava put her hand on Johanna's arm. "Have you ever walked a labyrinth?"

Johanna nodded. Dead ends could be deliberately designed.

"Let's just go a little further," Ava said. "If we don't have any . . . any good signs, then we walk back and make an opposite turn."

"No, let me go forward." She held up her hand. "I know what I said earlier about staying as a group. But I'm going to only go a short way and stay within hearing distance."

This time Ava motioned her head in agreement.

"Wait, you two. Let's give the old chair another try first," Eric said weakly. "This is a new type of tunnel. See the construction, the floors they're even. Push me up against the wall." He gave a thin smile. "The metal on the wheels is getting pretty battered. If we aren't heard, then we know the chances are this is not the one."

"Eric, but the pain it causes you," Ava said. "I can't do it."

"Then, Johanna, you're going to have to be the adult," Eric said. "Take the chair and push me alongside the wall." With a tightened jaw, he turned to look straight ahead. "Now."

Johanna reached for the chair handle.

The screech of the front wheel against the stone and the clatter of the arm handle breaking off, echoed into the darkness of the space, but it was not enough to cover Eric's scream.

TRINIDAD

THERE WAS A DISTANT NOISE—A CRASH? A scream? But from which direction? Trinidad's heart pounded.

"Johanna! Ava! Can you hear me?" Trinidad yelled into the darkness ahead.

She knew she had found them, but where to turn. She crawled past an open vent to storage room where she could see it only opened onto a new length of tunnel.

She hoped she would hear the sound again, but there was just silence. She kept crawling until she had to make a turn. Trinidad chose the passageway on the right. Not long after, there was distant rumbling overhead and voices—the police. She moved on until she ran out of her first roll of twine. Then she securely knotted the end to the start of the new roll. She made another turn to the right.

She sniffed when she came to a vent. Her heart once more raced. *Mi Fleur*, Leslie's perfume.

Trinidad crept along to the next vent opening. She turned on her phone's flashlight. It was a room, an empty room except for a sweater that lay on the floor—Leslie's sweater. Tears fell on her cheeks. She turned off the light to save the battery, and crawled forward taking the next turn to the right until she reached the next opening.

She took a big breath and yelled down the metal passage, "Johanna, Ava, can you hear me?"

Then from deep in the darkness.

"Trinidad, help! We hear you. Oh, my God, help!"

CHAPTER THIRTY-ONE

TRINIDAD STOOD OUTSIDE IN THE COOL NIGHT AIR next to the vent opening. Detective Quinn was clearly frustrated with her as he stood aside to let a slim woman wearing a lighted helmet, body heat sensor and rope, slip down to where Trinidad had emerged a short time before. A small group of officers were talking into their phones, moving into position.

"You sure you secured the twine on the other end?" She asked Trinidad, the majority of her body was already covered by the hole.

She nodded. "Yes, it is secure. When you smell perfume you will know you are close. I made all right turns."

The woman smiled. "Smart lady." She spoke into her shoulder mic, "Testing. I'm ready, let's go."

Quinn patted her on the back, signaling to go forward. And she was gone.

He turned to Trinidad, "I should charge you with obstruction of justice," Quinn said for the third time. "You could have put all our resources at risk trying to save you."

"I do not understand what your resources are, but I am glad you are here." She took a long swallow from the bottled water. "Detective Quinn, I apologize. I am not a . . . resource, but I would do again if it meant I could find Ava and Johanna."

No one was more surprised than Detective Nick Quinn and Trinidad when Eric Lowell was lifted through a tunnel at the rear of the house. Trinidad's eyes widened and she looked pointedly at Ava who only had eyes for her former husband.

"Eric Lowell, we thought you were dead," Quinn said. "For now, you're headed to the hospital, but when you're able we'll want to interview you."

Eric, eyes closed, nodded slightly. His strain and pain showed in the stretched straight-line of his lips.

"Please, he's barely conscious," Ava intervened. "Leave him be."

"Of course, Mrs. Lowell." Quinn said, stepping aside as the paramedics loaded Eric into the ambulance. "We're going to need a statement from you as well."

"Well, it won't be now. I'm going with him."

She wavered, almost slipping, trying to jump into the van and Quinn steadied her with a supporting hand.

"You're not well either. Make sure they look at you. I'll tell the officers to make sure you're checked out. Johanna said you were injected with some type of drug."

She gave him a grim smile and a nod. The doors closed, and the vehicle sped away.

Trinidad stared at Johanna as she gulped deeply from a bottle of water. They sat on the trunk opening of a police SUV. Emergency vehicle lights were flashing red and blue everywhere, and tall poles with spotlights had already been erected to scan the area in sweeping arcs.

"I was worried, Johanna. You do not always follow the rules," she said.

"And you do? Detective Quinn told me you had promised to stay in the car. He was not happy," she chided. "Trinidad, you could have been injured, traumatized, or even killed. I never . . . I never would have gotten over it."

"You don't have to, nothing happened. I am here." Trinidad pursed her lips. "To be correct, I only told Detective Quinn I understood he wanted me to stay. I didn't say I *would* stay. No matter, you and Ava are found. And Eric Lowell too, my heart could not believe. But the end is made up of means."

"The end justify the means." Johanna gave her a small smile.

"That is what I said." Trinidad frowned.

Kennedy brought mugs of coffee to a grateful Johanna and Trinidad. "Another ambulance is about five minutes away," he said. "We're going to need formal statements from both of you. Mrs. Hudson, did Carl Luden give you any idea where he might be headed?"

"No, my memory is a little cloudy right now, but I got the impression he had it all planned out. He wasn't making it up on the run. He knows where he's going. He has an escape tunnel in mind," Johanna said. "Agent Kennedy, have you found Leslie Todd?"

"Not yet." He shook his head. "We think she's with him. We took your advice Trin . . . Miss Owens and followed her perfume. There's a chance she left a trail on purpose. We put a trained dog down there, so we should get results soon. Mrs. Hudson, I was hoping you—"

He was interrupted by an anxious looking officer who motioned for him to move away so they could speak. Kennedy returned.

"They found Leslie Todd."

THE YOUNG WOMAN, SITTING ON A BOULDER, had been waiting next to the entrance of a tunnel exit. A police officer had covered her with a blanket and brought her to the gathering of law enforcement in front of the house. Leslie appeared disappointed and sad, but evidently not regretful enough to take on a new life with her grandfather.

Johanna heard the brief statement she gave to Nick. If Luden had told her his plan for disappearance, Leslie wasn't sharing it with the police. Although she did acknowledge her attempts to leave a trail of her perfume so they could locate Ava.

"I have to accept the fact my grandfather is a criminal." Leslie

added "Maybe he didn't pull the trigger on Phillip, but he con-
doned and encouraged his death."

"You seem pretty blasé about the killing of your fiancé," the
detective pointed out.

Leslie gave him a humorless smile. "You've got to believe me,
Phillip and I were done a long time ago. I just didn't deal with it.
I had no idea what my grandfather had in mind. He swore to me
Phillip's death was not his doing. I wanted to believe him," she said.
"At first, I had every intention of going with him, to be with my
only family. He told me my real family names and that I have two
uncles living in Illinois and a number of cousins." She smiled. "It
was so good to know that I have roots. I felt I could finally breathe."

She stopped.

"But?" Johanna prodded.

"But, he had no caring about Ava Lowell's kidnapping and
Johanna's treatment, they were innocents," she said. "When I saw
how his men handled and drugged Ava—I didn't want to live with
that on my conscience or be with someone, even my grandfather,
who was capable of doing such a thing. I had been searching all my
life for my history, I didn't want this horrific episode to be a part
of my future."

EPILOGUE

FOR NOW, THEY HADN'T FOUND CARL LUDEN. But this time
Leslie was working with law enforcement. Luden had revealed
his plans to his granddaughter in hopes of coaxing her to come
with him.

So much had taken place in just the past month, and that aus-
picious night. It was mid-week before a rested Johanna returned
to the office. When she greeted everyone on her return, Trinidad
hurried to reassure her that she and Marty had everything under
control.

"There is no need to worry," Trinidad insisted. "All our clients
are happy."

"I'm surprised we still have any clients," Johanna said. "I was too
loopy to answer emails, and when I got home my mother deliberately hid my phone."

"Are you kidding?" Marty said. "We have eight new clients
already signed up for appointments. I gave them our starter questionnaire to work on." He picked up a paper. "Take a look at the
log, Johanna, most of them are missing person cases. You're a
celebrity."

"I don't feel much like a celebrity," Johanna said, frowning at
the memory of the recent ordeal. "Missing persons, good grief. But

with Ava postponing her leaving for Australia and Eric's recovery, I am gaining back some feeling of a positive future. Speaking of Eric, I'm still in shock from his discovery."

"Me too." Trinidad tapped her head. "Oops, I forgot, Ava said to tell you she will be in late today. Eric Lowell is getting released from the hospital later this week, and she wants to make sure his condo is in good shape."

"I know, she called me last night."

Marty smiled. "Do you guys think Ava and Eric are getting back together?"

Trinidad and Johanna vigorously nodded.

"Hey, I'm glad for Ava," Marty said. "By the way, what are we going to do with that machine we bought her, the . . . the Total Station?"

Johanna's brow wrinkled. "Hmm, good question. I had forgotten about the dig . . . 'er thing. It's taking up all the spare space in the break room. Let's give it to Ava when she gets here and see how she wants to handle it."

Marty remarked to Johanna and Trinidad that Leslie Todd had sent in a sizable check to more than cover Legacy's expenses. "She gave us a pretty comfortable tip."

"Luden told me she had her own money through Leslie's mother estate," Johanna said. "Hopefully, after facing her past demons, she can fill in the missing links in her life and move forward to finding peace of mind."

"Then, with the extra money I think we may have to rent the space next door," Trinidad replied. "To make room for the dig machine."

They all laughed.

"Well, it's good to hear laughter from this place for once," Nick Quinn said, walking into the room followed by Agent Kennedy. They stood just inside the doorway. "We stopped by to say thank you for all you did to help us catch some very bad men. The drones lit them up like Christmas bulbs as they tried to run.

Thanks to you, we captured all but one member of Luden's conspiracy team."

"Come in, you two," Johanna said directing them to the chairs in the conference room. "I take it Luden was the one who got away."

"For now, but he'll resurface again," Kennedy said. "The money we gave him to go for protection has numbers we can track. He won't get far before he realizes and is faced with limited resources. He'll be trying to launder it."

"Detective, I notice you do not sound surprised when you heard Eric Lowell was alive," Trinidad said as a statement and not a question. "You knew he was not dead or disappeared all this time. Why did you play such a horrible trick on us?"

Marty nodded. "Yeah."

"She's right," Johanna said. "You knew all along he was still alive."

Nick Quinn held up his hands as if in surrender.

"All right, all right, Lowell was working with us, sort of, to nail Carl Luden," Detective Quinn said. "But we didn't know where he was. He had some dumb idea to get Luden to confess to Nava's murder, and he was sure he could get a read on where Luden had access to the illegal money. He wanted to impress you, and us, with his new persona—a changed man. We stopped him before he screwed up our plans and convinced him to play just a small role for us as an informant. Only they kidnapped him before we could get any evidence. It was important we went along with the farce if we wanted him kept alive."

"Fortunately for you he was missing only a few days. There was no need to build a story for his family. Bet you were nervous when he disappeared." Johanna said.

"There has not been a dull moment in this whole matter," Nick Quinn acknowledged. "Maybe now you can see why we do not like to work with civilians. And yes, we have since told his family he is in good hands. Ava has been in touch with them too."

Kennedy accepted a cup of coffee from Marty.

He added, "When Luden ducked the protection program ten years ago, he took all the ill-gotten gains with him, we thought," Kennedy declared. "But he had turned in only the dollars to satisfy entry into the protection program. Afterwards, we found out through our field agents there was even more money he had held on to. That's when he dropped out of the program and went rogue. Without going into a lot of detail, we had to protect our lines of communication. He hid the money and didn't touch a dollar until a few months ago."

"I guess you thought you would just wait until he took the bait," Johanna said. "But, not to rub it in, it wasn't until Legacy Consultants brought you Leslie Todd that you actually found him."

IT WAS LATER THAT WEEK WHEN JOHANNA GAZED down at her phone. She couldn't stop the silly smile that played on her lips. Nick's invitation to dinner was not a surprise—what was a surprise was the change of clothes and toothbrush he left behind in the second bathroom.

Ava sat across from her in their conference room and sported an amused smile. "Let me guess, the engaging Detective Quinn is finally making his move. It took him long enough."

"You should talk, Ava. How is Eric doing?"

This time it was Ava's turn to check out her own fingernails. "He's on his way back to normal. The eye surgery yesterday was a success. Recovery will take a while, but he'll keep his sight. His leg operations righted everything that wasn't—so he's going to be okay."

"Tell me, what he was thinking to get himself so embroiled in this mess. What was his plan?"

"He tells me he was working with the I.R.S.—Kennedy's people. He basically verified what Agent Kennedy had already told us. Frankly, I also think Eric has probably cut a deal with his taxes." Ava crossed her arms. "He doesn't want to talk about how they treated him in capture. I think he got the crap scared out of him."

"Has it changed him?"

"I don't know." Ava raised an eyebrow. "Hopefully he's scared straight. I spoke with his family and they said he had already talked with them and apologized for putting them through any worry and made arrangements for his mother to spend time with him. The old Eric would never have done that. They are surprised, too."

Johanna leaned over the table and held Ava's hand. "As horrible as this awful incident was, maybe there's good also."

"Maybe." She gave her friend a small smile. "He said when he realized where they had taken him, he thought they were leaving him to die."

"But he didn't."

"No, he didn't." Ava paused. "I never realized how much he was still a part of me, and now I have some thinking to do."

"Oh, Ava, I'm so glad to hear that. And what about the two of you—together I mean."

"We'll see."

JOHANNA HAD OFFERED MARTY THE CHANCE to step up and assist new clients with completing their questionnaire. He declined.

"Nah, but thanks Johanna. I'm okay with being a receptionist and running errands to the court house. I'm really interested in continuing my private investigator training classes. I could be even more help to you if I have a license especially if we're going to be focusing on family trees with missing persons."

She grinned.

"True. Then you let me know if you need help earning practice hours. I know a couple of people who might be interested in having an apprentice."

IT WAS TRINIDAD WHO CAUSED THE MOST raised eyebrows in the office. She had changed her wardrobe to include classic pant suits and even skirts—in attractive colors that suited her tawny skin tone and dark hair. Over the next week, she took over more of the assistant role for clients, ready to walk them through the mapping to reveal ancestors.

"You must be going somewhere," Johanna observed. "That outfit suits you. Teal is definitely your color."

Marty looked up. "Perhaps the look is for Agent Kennedy," he teased. "I think I overheard something about a lunch? Or, was it a dinner?"

Trinidad gave him a razor look and had opened her mouth to retort, until the subject of the conversation walked into the lobby.

Paul Kennedy's generous smile was only for her.

"Hi there," he said. "I have to make a late meeting at a field office nearby, so my assistant gave me this parcel for you, Mrs. Hudson. It contains your belongings left behind in the Napa house." He handed Johanna a small package. "Ready for lunch, Trinidad? I know I'm a little early."

She nodded quickly.

Johanna grinned, noticing Trinidad's surprising look of shyness. "Thank you, Agent Kennedy, good to see you. One thing I learned from these past weeks is the world of detecting is not boring."

"Yes, it is good to finally know how things end up," Trinidad said. "The grass is also brown on the other side."

Johanna opened her mouth to correct her, but stopped.

Kennedy's eyes went to Trinidad's. "Absolutely."

And Trinidad beamed.

R. **Franklin James grew up in the** San Francisco Bay Area, graduated from UC Berkeley, and flourished in a career of public policy and political advocacy. In 2013, the first book in her five-star Hollis Morgan Mystery Series, *The Fallen Angels Book Club*, was published by Camel Press it was followed by *Sticks & Stones, The Return of the Fallen Angels Book Club, The Trade List, The Bell Tolls* and *The Identity Thief*. In 2022 the six book series was acquired by Lifetime/A&E and successfully adapted into two TV movies released in the US and globally. In 2019 her book, *The Appraiser* was published in 2019. *The Inheritance*, the first book in her Johanna Hudson series was released in April 2021, followed by *Look Twice* in 2022. James resides in northern California with her husband.

www.ingramcontent.com/pod-product-compliance
Lightning Source LLC
Chambersburg PA
CBHW011516100726
47899CB00010BD/3382